TIGER,
TIGER

TIGER, TIGER

Lynne Reid Banks

HarperCollins *Children's Books*

First published in Great Britain by HarperCollins *Children's Books* 2004
This edition published by HarperCollins *Children's Books* 2005
HarperCollins *Children's Books* is an imprint of HarperCollins*Publishers* Ltd,
77-85 Fulham Palace Road, Hammersmith, London W6 8JB

The HarperCollins *Children's Books* website address is
www.harpercollinschildrensbooks.co.uk

1 3 5 7 9 8 6 4 2

Text copyright © Lynne Reid Banks 2004

Lynne Reid Banks asserts the moral right to be identified as the author of this work.

ISBN 0 00 772595 7

Printed and bound in England by
Clays Ltd, St Ives plc

For my son, Gillon Stephenson.

CONTENTS

PROLOGUE

The two tiger cubs, romping in the jungle undergrowth near their den, prick up their ears.

While they play by themselves, they always half listen for their mother's return. But these sounds are not what they want to hear. They are strange and alarming. Loud, staccato beats, clattering and banging – hacking and chopping – a trampling of green stems. And voices. Not animal voices, all familiar to them. These are voices alien to the jungle. And when they begin, other sounds, the sounds that make a constant, reassuring background to the cubs' lives, fall silent.

They look around, anxiously. Something is coming. Where is their mother?

As the barrage of noise gets nearer, there is a sudden wild whirring over their heads. They look up, and see a blur of colour and affrighted movement as a flock of birds takes flight, disturbing the leaves.

Next, bands of monkeys go fleeing hand over hand through the canopy above, chattering and screaming in terror.

It is a signal. Beasts that have been hiding, spring up. The cubs see a buck stumbling clumsily among the trees, not far from them. At a greater distance, they hear an elephant trumpet a warning. Smaller creatures flee invisibly but audibly through the undergrowth. Every sound they hear seems to urge them to run. But they do not. The flight instinct conflicts with their mother's training – they must stay by the den, where she can find them.

They crouch together, keeping low. There is a brief pause. Then suddenly the line of hunters breaks through the jungle thickets into the small clearing in front of the den.

The bigger cub tries to run now, but it is too late.

He is pounced on, seized by the scruff of the neck, and thrust into a sack. He squirms and squeals and tries to bite his captor, but it is useless. The smaller cub doesn't even manage to struggle – he is enclosed in a dark, noisome place, and swung upward. They can see nothing now, but they hear the sound of trampling underneath them, and the ear-hurting other sounds fade. They are bumped up and down, their bodies distressed, their minds blank with bewilderment.

The two hunters who carry the sacks reach the edge of the forest where their horses wait. They hand their burdens to others while they mount, then take the sacks again and loop them over the pommels of their saddles.

The horses can smell the tiger-scent and begin neighing and curvetting, trying to get away from it. Their skilled riders use this fear to urge them forward. The tigress, they know, cannot be far away.

Behind them, in the jungle, the noise of the beaters continues. More beasts are being hunted and trapped.

The moment their heads are freed, the horses rear up, then gallop for the riverbank, where the boats wait.

With their goal in sight, the riders' hair stands suddenly on end as they hear behind them the ferocious roar of a charging tiger. The horses bolt. Reaching the ramp that connects the bank with the first boat, the leading horse bounds up it. The one behind utters a scream as it feels the tigress's claws tear its haunch – then, wild-eyed, it plunges up on to the deck.

The hunters disengage the sacks and fling them

expertly to the waiting sailors. Then they jump from their horses, and turn at the rail to watch as others repel their pursuer.

As the cubs are carried down to where cages wait in the grim bowels of the ship, they cannot know that their last chance of rescue lies at the foot of the gangway with a spear through her heart.

CHAPTER ONE

In the Hold

The two cubs huddled together, their front paws intertwined, their heads and flanks pressed to each other.

Darkness crushed them, and bad smells, and motion. And fear.

The darkness was total. It was not what they were used to. In the jungle there is always light for a tiger's eyes. It filters down through the thickest leaves from a generous sky that is never completely dark. It reflects off pools and glossy leaves and the eyes of other creatures. Darkness in the jungle is a reassurance. It says it's time to come out of the lair, to play, to eat, to learn the night.

It's a safe darkness, a familiar, *right* darkness. This darkness was all wrong.

The smells were bad because there was no way to bury their scat. And there was the smell of other animals, and their fear. And there was a strange smell they didn't recognise, a salt smell like blood. But it wasn't blood.

It was bad being enclosed. All the smells that should have dissipated on the wind were held in, close. Cloying the sensitive nostrils. Choking the breath. Confusing and deceiving, so that the real smells, the smells that mattered, couldn't be found, however often the cubs put up their heads and reached for them, sniffing in the foul darkness.

The motion was the worst. The ground under them was not safe and solid. It pitched and rocked. Sometimes it leant so far that they slid helplessly until they came up against something like hard, cold, thin trees. These were too close together to let the cubs squeeze between them. Next moment the ground tipped the other way. The cubs slid though the stinking straw till they fell against the cold trees on the other side. When the unnatural motion grew really strong, the whole enclosure they were in slid and crashed against other hard things, frightening the cubs so that they snarled and panted and clawed at the hard non-earth under their pads, trying in vain to steady themselves.

They would put back their heads and howl, and try to bite the cold thin things that stopped them being free. Then their slaver sometimes had blood in it.

When the awful pitching and rolling stopped and they could once again huddle up close, their hearts stopped racing, and they could lick each other's faces for reassurance.

They were missing their mother – their Big One. They waited for her return – she had always come back before. But she was gone for ever. No more warm coat, no rough, comforting, cleansing tongue. No more good food, no big body to clamber on, no tail to chase, pretending it was prey. No more lessons. No more love and safety.

All their natural behaviour was held in abeyance. They no longer romped and played. There was no space and they had no spirit for it. Mostly they lay together and smelt each other's good smell through all the bad smells.

As days and nights passed in this terrifying, sickening fashion, they forgot their mother, because only Now mattered for them. Now's bewilderment, fear, helplessness and disgust.

There was only one good time in all the long hours. They came to look forward to it, to know when it was coming.

They began to recognise when the undifferentiated thudding overhead, where the sky ought to be, presaged the opening of a piece of that dead sky, and the descent from this hole of the two-legged male animals that brought them food. Then they would jump to their feet and mewl and snarl with excitement and eagerness. They would stretch their big paws through the narrow space between the cold trees and, when the food came near, try to hook it with their claws and draw it close more quickly. The food, raw meat on a long, flat piece of wood, would be shoved through a slot down near the ground, the meat – never quite enough to fill their stomachs – scraped off, and the wood withdrawn. Water came in a bowl through the same slot. They often fought over it and spilt it. They were nearly always thirsty.

The male two-legs made indecipherable noises: "Eat up, boys! Eat and grow and get strong. You're going to need it, where you're going!"

And then there would be a sound like a jackal's yelping and the two-legs would move off and feed the other creatures imprisoned in different parts of the darkness.

Brown bears. Jackals. A group of monkeys, squabbling and chattering hysterically. There were wild dogs, barking incessantly and giving off a terrible stench of anger and fear. There were peacocks with huge rustling tails, that spoke in screeches. And somewhere quite far away, a she-elephant, with something fastened to her legs that made an unnatural clanking sound as she shifted her great body from foot to foot in the creaking, shifting, never-ending dark.

One night the dogs began to bite and tear at each other amid an outburst of snarling and shrieking sounds. The cubs were afraid and huddled down in the farthest corner of their prison. But they could hear the wild battles as one dog after another succumbed and was torn to pieces. The next time the sky opened, the two-legged animals found a scene of carnage, with only two dogs left alive.

"There'll be trouble now," one muttered, as he dragged the remains out from a half-opening while others held the survivors off with pointed sticks.

"I said they should have put 'em all in separate cages. They'll say we didn't feed 'em enough."

"Better cut the corpses up and give the meat to the tigers. Dogs is one thing, but if we lose one of them cubs, we'll be dog meat ourselves."

After that there was no shortage of food and the cubs spent most of the time when they weren't eating, sleeping off their huge meals. But their sleep was not peaceful.

The cubs had no desire to fight or kill each other. They didn't know they were brothers, but each knew that the other was all he had. One was the first-born and the larger. He was the leader. In the jungle, he had been fed first and most, and had led their games and pretend hunts. He was also the more intelligent of the two. He came to understand that it was no use howling and scratching at the ground and rubbing backwards and forwards with cheek and sides against the cold, close-together barriers, or trying to chew them to pieces. When his brother did these things, he would knock him down with his paw and lie on him to stop him.

The younger one would submit. It was better, he found. His paws, throat and teeth stopped being sore. He learnt to save his energies. But the misery was still there. It only stopped while he ate, and when he curled up with his brother and they licked each other's faces, and slept.

At last it ended.

The sky-hole opened and stayed open and a new

smell came through. They smelt earth and vegetation – not what they'd been used to, but bearing some comforting relation to it.

They stood together side by side, alert and waiting for what would happen next. The two-legged animals were running about over their heads and making loud noises with their mouths. The sky-hole grew bigger, and at last they could see the blue of the real sky over their heads. Something came down from above, grasped their prison and swung it upwards! It rocked and swayed and the cubs fell on their sides and couldn't get up without falling down again. After a short journey, there was a hard jolt. Then two-legged ones gathered around them, peering at them, their loud mouth-noises coming from all directions.

One of them put its long-toed hairless paw in between the thin trees. The bigger cub snarled and snapped at it furiously. It was snatched away and there was an outcry.

"It tried to bite me!"

"Stupid! What do you expect? It's wild, it's not used to being petted."

"But they look so sweet, like big kittens—"

"Do you need to lose half your hand to find out that they're not? They're for the arena, they have to be fierce."

The cubs watched warily as the other captives were lowered to the ground near them, and soon the crowd had moved away to inspect the bears, the peacocks, the monkeys. When the she-elephant was carefully lowered from above, there were gasps and shouts.

"Great gods! What a size! Keep clear of it!"

"Will the Emperor show it at the Colosseum? Will they bait it, like the bears, with dogs?"

"Perhaps. I hope so! What a fabulous show that would be!"

"How many dogs will it take to kill a thing that size?"

"No, Caesar won't have it baited or killed. They never kill the elephants. Perhaps he'll ride on it. Think of that! Our great Emperor on the tallest beast in the world, riding along the Appian Way! What a triumph!"

Thick vines were joined to the cubs' prison and by them it was dragged on to the back of some unalive thing that nonetheless moved. It was pulled by animals whose feet made a hard, clattering sound against the ground. The cubs looked about them. There was sunlight, but not filtered through greenery. It flooded unhindered over green and yellow stretches of ground. The tigers had never left the jungle, never seen fields and crops, and these puzzled them, but at least it was natural earth and growing things – they could smell them and they longed to be free to bound away and seek safety and a hiding place. Freedom was something they had not forgotten.

Behind them came the other captives, dragged along like them. The bears, on their hind legs, held the prison-trees and roared at the crowd. The jackals pawed and whined. The monkeys leapt about, twisting their heads and gazing here and there with their little bright eyes. The two surviving dogs lay licking their wounds. The elephant stood swaying on her huge feet.

The motion went on for a long time. After a while, the cubs grew tired and lay down and slept.

When they woke up, they saw that the natural scenes had gone. Now they could understand nothing of what they saw. They were moving among many two-legs and behind these were big cliffs of stone that had caves in them where two-legs were passing in and out, or standing in the higher ones, looking out. Their interesting but nose-wrinkling smell and the noise of their mouths were everywhere.

The cubs dangled their tongues and let the scent of warm edible flesh enter their noses.

Chapter Two

Caesar's Daughter

The Lady Aurelia was reclining on a couch on the balcony of her bedroom. She was twelve years old but already so beautiful and womanly that her father, the Emperor, had issued a protective edict that no man might be alone in her presence without his express permission. The balcony overlooked the palace gardens, and beyond them, three of Rome's fabled "seven hills" could be seen, covered with a mixture of sun-bleached stone buildings and Cyprus trees, their stately dark fingers wagging at the sky as if admonishing the gods for not giving Aurelia enough to do.

Her mother had hinted again, only that morning,

that Aurelia was indulging in too much idleness and daydreaming. As a Roman emperor's daughter she already had some duties, but they were not of a kind to alleviate the boredom she felt in doing them or in looking ahead to doing them again tomorrow. She had her regular lessons, of course, but only the musical ones actually engaged her, and that was as much because of the charms of her music teacher, a young Assyrian with coal-black curly hair and nervous but excited eyes, as for any fascination with the lute. Her other tutors were old and deadly dull, and didn't seem to realise that she was quicker-witted than they were, and usually grasped what they were mumbling at her long before they'd got to the end of their meandering sentences.

Aurelia had all the intelligence that her clever parents could bequeath her. But it seemed it wasn't going to do her much good.

Of course, her looks would do her good, if being helped to a rich husband was considered good. The son of a senator, perhaps, or an officer in the Praetorian Guard. She was aware that her mother was already on the lookout for a suitable match, though she would not be expected to marry until she was thirteen, or even fourteen if she were lucky.

She sighed from her very depths. Other young girls

23

– the few her parents considered suitable for her to associate with – seemed to talk and think of little but beautiful young men and marriage, but to Aurelia the idea of following in her mother's footsteps – marriage at thirteen, motherhood a year later, a life of matronly duties and domesticity – appealed to Aurelia about as strongly as being tied up in the arena and fed to the wild beasts, like those strange, death-inviting Christians.

No, no. Of course not, not *that*. Aurelia stopped sighing and shuddered. She turned her mind away, accompanying the mental trick with a swift quarter-turn of her head. She had learnt early how to swamp ugly imaginings with pleasant ones.

"I am so lucky, not to be a Christian," she said aloud. This was part of the ritual of drowning fearful or unpleasant thoughts.

She was lucky. She had grown up knowing that she was. This was part of her cleverness, because others in her fortunate situation might have taken it entirely for granted, and not bothered comparing themselves with others. But from her earliest childhood Aurelia had observed the difference between the way she lived and the way the common people of Rome lived, in their several social layers, right to the bottom where there were slaves and the poor. It was a very great difference, and she pondered it every time she left the palace.

Even inside it, the palace servants, though relatively comfortable, led lives of terrifying insecurity. Once, five years ago, she had seen one of her own handmaids cruelly flogged. It had happened as a direct result of Aurelia complaining about her for some trifle. When a young child witnesses such a thing and knows herself to be the cause, she learns some lessons. The simplest would be to harden her heart. That's what others did. But Aurelia learnt something better – to control her temper and to deal with her servants herself.

But she had learnt something more from hearing her maid's screams. She had found out her place in the world, that she had power, and that her father had much more – almost an infinite amount. Later she grasped something of what power means. What she didn't yet understand was why some have it and others lie under its lash. If her tutors could have taught her *that*, she would have listened to them with all her attention. But when she asked them, they seemed not only unwilling, but unable to answer. Some of her questions scandalised them.

"All societies have hierarchies," she was told. "All societies have higher and lower, masters and slaves."

"It must be terrible to be a slave!"

"You must not entertain such thoughts. Waste no pity on slaves. They have no responsibilities, no traditions to maintain, no laws to make and keep. They have no concerns about food and shelter. They only have to do what they're told, and live out their simple lives in peace and order."

"And the animals?"

"What animals?"

"For example, the animals in the arena that are set to fight the gladiators, and each other. They're usually killed in the end, and they've done no wrong. Why do they have to be hurt?"

Her teacher stared at her.

"Why does any living being suffer? It is all the will of the gods. It is their design. It is blasphemy to question the order of nature. Surely you're not questioning your father's right to show the people signs of his power, to entertain them with circuses?"

Aurelia was silent. But on another occasion, she asked: "What is Christianity? Why is it so dangerous that people are killed for it?"

This time her tutor threw up his hands. "Don't you know that Christians don't believe in our gods – that they've set up a single, all-powerful god above ours? Could any heresy be worse? Come, enough of this idle tongue-wagging! You must stop asking foolish questions and get down to the study of the heavens." He wagged a finger at her. "Sometimes it is hard not to suspect *you* of harbouring heretical thoughts."

Heretical thoughts. Thoughts outside what was permitted.

Aurelia knew she had many such thoughts and questions. With good reason this simple fact terrified her, and she tried to suppress them. Even being Caesar's daughter would not save her from some dreadful punishment if it was believed she criticised him, even in the privacy of her heart.

Now she rose languidly and walked slowly through the heat to the fountain in the centre of the courtyard of her apartment. Its constant music and the cooler air around it always soothed her. In the pool at the fountain's foot there were water lilies, and in their shadow exotic fish, brought from afar. She crouched beside the parapet and trailed her hot hand in the limpid water, letting the tinkle and splash of the fountain make her mind a harmless blank.

A large orange-coloured fish came to nose her fingers inquisitively.

She did her trick, something she'd discovered for

herself. She let her fingers move gently in the water, and the fish glided in between them and held itself there with lazy motions of its tail while she very delicately stroked its slippery sides. She concentrated intently. She knew that if she moved her hand quickly enough she could stick her forefinger and thumb into the fish's gills and, in a swift movement, lift it out of the water. She could capture it and end its life if she chose to. She knew this because she'd done it once, held a trapped fish firmly out of the water, felt it struggling in her hands, felt its struggles cease... Afterwards she'd felt sick. She'd thrown the dead thing back in the pond, where it turned on its side and floated until a servant came and cleared it away.

Now she tickled the fish for a few minutes and then lifted her hand suddenly and watched it flash away amid the bright drops from her fingers.

That was power. To have a life in your hand. Even a fish's. She felt the thrill of it. But something told her it was an evil power – to kill because you could, without reason, for pleasure. She felt dimly that the true power was to withhold the death-stroke, to let the creature go when you *could* have killed it.

Such deep thoughts tired her. She sighed and went back to her day bed.

She had hardly settled on it when one of her maids came soft-footedly across the marble tiles to her side. She was breathing fast and her face was flushed.

"My lady, someone is here to see you. He – he has brought a gift." She looked strange, as if she were torn between hysterical laughter, and fear.

Aurelia sat up sharply.

"Who is it?"

"I don't know. But he says your honourable father sent him."

"Well, send him in!"

"No – no, I can't, my lady! You must come out and see what he's brought. He can't bring it in here!" She let out a high-pitched giggle of excitement.

Aurelia pulled the girl down beside her. "Tell me," she said. "Tell me at once what it is."

"It's – it's a..."

"Yes, go on! What's the matter with you?"

"It's a *tiger*, my lady!"

Aurelia was silent for a moment, puzzled.

"You mean, a tiger-skin rug."

"No."

"A stuffed tiger."

"No, my lady! A real, live one! Oh, please come and see it!"

Aurelia pushed her away, threw her long dark curling hair back over her shoulders, and stood up. Her heart was throbbing behind her ribs. A *real, live* tiger? But that was impossible! Of all the beasts brought from far-off countries to please the crowds with their ferocity, the tiger was one of the most formidable. Also, because it came, not from Africa, but from some far eastern land, it was the rarest, and most terrible, somehow. There could be no one bold enough to introduce one into Caesar's palace! But the girl had said Aurelia's father had sent it. As a *gift*

She ran swiftly across the cool floor to the double doorway and flung the doors open.

There it was, indeed. Safely in a cage on wheels. And very young. And very, very — oh, there were no words for what it was! Beautiful, sweet, adorable. Fabulous.

Aurelia didn't even notice the person who had brought it. She crouched down, a safe distance from the cage, and stared into the yellow eyes of the cub.

"Hello," she breathed.

The cub stared back for about five seconds. Then it turned its face aside.

One paw, seemingly too large for its body, stuck through the bars of its cage. Not the whole paw, of course — the bars were too close together. Just the tip of it. Aurelia, greatly daring, crept forward and touched the golden fur with one finger. The cub pulled the paw back and then swiped the bars of the cage. Aurelia saw its claws spread themselves and jerked her hand away.

"He wants to scratch me!"

"It's his instinct, Princess. But don't fear. His claws will be seen to."

She looked up swiftly. He was young and brown with smooth, round, muscled arms. A slave from the menagerie. He wore an animal skin over his tunic as a sign of his profession.

"'Seen to'? How, seen to?"

"His claws will be drawn."

She frowned. "What do you mean, drawn?"

"Pulled out, Princess."

For a second she felt faint. She clenched her hands as a sympathetic pain struck her fingernails.

"You mean – someone will pull out all his claws?"

"Of course. You couldn't play with him if he had sharp claws."

"How? How will they do it?"

"You need not trouble yourself—"

She raised her voice to one of command. "Tell me immediately how they will... draw his claws?"

"With pliers, my lady. They will pull them out as teeth are pulled out."

She stood up. "You will not do that to him. You will cut his claws instead, the way my finger and toenails are cut by my maid, straight across so they have no sharp points."

"He could still—"

"There is no more to be said. He is to be mine, isn't that so? I will say what shall be done with him."

The young keeper bowed his head. But still, he muttered something.

"Speak louder!"

"I said, Princess, that you may keep him in his cage, just as he is, but if you want to let him out and play with him, you must let us protect you. He's only a baby now, but like a cat he can already bite and scratch." He showed her several deep red scratches on his arm. She drew in her breath. "And when he grows a little bigger he may be dangerous to you unless you let us draw his claws. His fangs," he added boldly, "have already been removed."

"What!" she shouted. "You've started pulling his teeth out too! How will he eat?"

"Our concern," said the youth, with a touch of humour, "is that he shall not eat *you*."

She looked back at the cub. He was looking at her again.

"Will he try to bite me if I put my hand into his cage?"

"No. I have handled him and gentled him. Also he's not feeling very fierce just now because of the long journey he's had, and the operation. Do you like him?"

"Oh, *yes*," she breathed, gazing at the fabulous creature. Her own. Her very own. She glanced again at the scratches on the young man's smooth, brown arm, and quailed for a moment. But then she stiffened herself. Cautiously she stretched her small hand, sideways to be narrow enough, between two bars towards the animal's bicoloured head. Its ears moved, flattened. It growled deep in its throat. She snatched her hand out again.

The young keeper laughed. He unfastened the lid at the top of the cage and raised it. Then he reached in fearlessly and scratched the cub behind the ears. It looked up at him trustingly.

"How can he like you and trust you when you've hurt him? It must have hurt terribly to have his fangs pulled out!"

"I didn't do it, Princess. I was the one who comforted him afterwards, rubbed oil of cloves on the wounds and gave him warm milk in a bottle to remind him of his mother."

"Where is she?"

"Who knows? Far away in the jungle he came from. He won't see her again." He was petting and stroking the tiger's head, working his hand under its jaw. The cub's eyes closed in bliss. There was a different sound from him now – a rumble of pleasure.

Aurelia stood up. "Oh, let me! Only I don't want him to growl at me."

"He won't. Here, take over from me. He'll soon learn to accept you."

The cub's warm fur was a delight – so soft, so silky-soft, such beautiful colours, rich gold and deep, dark black. After a tentative moment, she sank her fingers into it luxuriantly and was overjoyed when the cub continued to purr like the great cat that he was. She was soon using both hands to pet and please him. Better than stroking a fish!

The keeper-boy was talking.

"He's a present from your father. There were two of them, twin brothers. One, the bigger and stronger of the two, has been taken to the Colosseum to be raised for the circus. This one was chosen as a special pet for you by the Emperor."

Aurelia withdrew her hands and stood staring down at the baby tiger, who followed her now with his yellow eyes.

"Do I have to keep him always in a cage? Because if so, I don't want him."

"Well, I can take him out now, if you like. We'll see if he behaves himself, but I don't think he will try any tricks while I'm here."

When she nodded breathlessly, he reached down and lifted the cub out of the cage, talking to him in a clucking, rumbling tone. He held him, positively cuddling him. Aurelia's arms ached to hold the furry adorable thing.

"Good boy. You're a lucky cub. Look at your mistress! Wasn't that worth a little pain? You're better off than your brother!" And he lowered him on to his big, padded feet on the marble floor, where he stood, his tail twitching from side to side.

"Does he understand what you say to him?"

"No. But it soothes him. You must talk to him a lot. And you must learn his language."

"Does he *talk*?" she asked naively.

He smiled. "Yes, in his own way. Look at his tail, now. If it were lashing from side to side, you'd need to be careful, because that means, *I am angry! I may pounce!*

But that twitching is just uncertainty – curiosity."

"No, no! Tell me exactly what he's saying!"

"He's saying, *I don't know where I am or what's happening. Reassure me. Be kind to me. Tell me I'm safe.*"

"Oh! Yes, I see!" Aurelia, enchanted, fell on her knees and put out both her arms to the cub. "Come here to me! I won't hurt you. I love you already. Come and be stroked!" But the cub stood still and didn't come. She looked up beseechingly at the young keeper. "What can I say to him to make him come?"

"Nothing. You must offer him a gift."

"What? What?"

The keeper opened a basket he had on his back and took from it a small piece of raw meat.

"Are you afraid to get your hands soiled?"

She hesitated, but only for a moment. "No! Give it to me!"

He handed her the meat. Before she fully had hold of it, the cub leapt forward and snatched it from her grasp, startling her so much she cried out and fell over backwards. In a moment, the young man had his hand fastened on the scruff of the cub's neck and it shrank down. But Aurelia sat up at once and said, "No, he didn't mean to frighten me. Leave him."

The keeper obeyed. The cub lay down and began

chewing on the meat. Every now and then he shook his head.

"Why does he do that?"

"He can't understand why he can't eat quite as he used to. And it may still hurt a little."

Aurelia crept towards him.

"No, my lady," warned the keeper. "Don't try to touch him while he's eating. He'll think—" He corrected himself. "Look, he's put his ears back. He's saying, *Don't try to take my food!* When he's satisfied his hunger he'll remember that you gave him the meat. He may sniff the blood on your hand, and come to lick it off. Then he'll begin to recognise you. That's how cats are. They like you for what you give them."

"I want him to love me for myself."

"Better not to hope for that. He'll be your companion, but never will he love you. Cats can't love, except perhaps each other. But be kind to him and learn his language and you can be friends, in a way."

Aurelia sat on the floor with her diaphanous robes spread about her, and watched the cub eat. She didn't move a muscle till he had finished. Then, as he was licking his whiskers, she said, "Can I keep him with me all the time? Can he sleep in my bed?"

The youth shook his head.

"I am to stay with you while you get acquainted. Then he must go back in his cage and I will take him back to the menagerie for the night. You have other things to do. But he'll look forward to coming to see you, to leaving his cage, to eating from your hand, to being petted, to being free. In that way he'll become yours."

"Has he a name?"

"I call him Tigris."

"But that's just what he is! That's a boring name."

"Then think of a better one, Princess."

She looked at the cub a long time. He stared at her, but he did not come to lick her hand. She wiped it on the floor.

"I'll spend the night thinking," she said.

The young man bent and picked the cub up. "I must take him now."

"Can I kiss him?"

He smiled secretly, thinking: *Fortunate creature.* "Yes. Why not?"

Aurelia came close and kissed the cub on the head and touched his hurt face tenderly. "Goodbye, little one. When you come back to me tomorrow, I will have a name for you."

She watched as he was put back in his cage and

wheeled away. The young man looked back once, irresistibly, but she didn't notice. Her mind was following the tiger – her tiger – and was busy with the delightful task of naming him.

"What's your name?" she called after the youth.

"Julius."

"Come early, Julius!"

"Willingly!" he said, and added, in his head, *If only your eagerness were for me!*

CHAPTER THREE

The Naming

The younger and smaller cub, still lacking a name, spent the night alone in his cage, in the city menagerie where he was to live.

His brain was full of new things, new bewilderments. Having his fangs drawn had been terrible, but the pain was fading and with it the memory of his terror and agony. He thought about the male two-legs that had comforted him, making soft sounds to him and giving him milk to suck, reminding him dimly of his lost Big One. Not all two-legs were either things to fear or things he might like to eat. They were certainly meat, but they were more. They were powerful and puzzling and even fearsome, but also they could do pleasing things. He thought of the female two-legs with the eyes that had looked into his. He had wanted to creep to her and lick the blood off her hand after she had provided him with food, encourage that hand to scratch and stroke him again. He sensed no threat, but he was uncertain. He hadn't seen anything like her before.

Where was his brother?

That was the most important thing.

They had been a pair, and now that had ended and he was alone. In the darkness there was no warm, friendly other to curl up against. No familiar smell and no one to communicate with.

He slept at last, miserable, aching and lonely.

But in the morning things were better. The male two-legs came and made sounds to him and petted him. There were others with him, but the cub only noticed the one he knew.

"Today would have been a bad day for you, Tigris, but you're lucky again. She's forbidden it. So I've got something for you instead, so that you won't forget yourself and do her a mischief!" He reached down into the cage and began to rub the cub's belly. Instinctively he rolled over and stuck his big feet in the air. Before he understood what was happening, something was slipped over each of them, something that muffled his claws.

He rolled over swiftly and stood up, sniffing this new addition to his body. He didn't like it. He caught the stuff in his teeth and tried to pull it off, but he couldn't. It fitted tightly around his legs and was too strong to tear.

He rolled and rubbed and bit, but it was useless. The young two-legs watched him, and, when he could, scratched the cub's ears.

"Get used to it, friend. You're a *shod* tiger now, and you must wear them till you learn good manners. Till you can be trusted."

"If that day ever comes!" said one of the others.

But the cub understood only that when he tried to walk he couldn't properly feel the ground under his feet and learn from it. He didn't yet know that he couldn't use his claws. But when his day's meat was brought to him, he found out. He was used to pinning the meat down with his claws and chewing chunks off it. But this meat was in small pieces. He didn't realise that it was because his jaws ached too much to chew properly. All he knew was that he couldn't hold it, he couldn't rend it... He was no longer whole, no longer what he had been. What he knew he was meant to be. He was muffled. He was less.

★

When he was taken to the female two-legs, he was already angry.

She took one look at him and began to make a mouth-noise.

"Oh, look! He's got boots on!"

"Yes, Princess. It was Caesar's orders when he heard that you'd forbidden us to draw his claws."

She capered about joyfully.

"I couldn't think of a name for him, but now I have it! I'll call him Boots!"

The cub named Boots without knowing he'd been named, watched her, surprised because she whirled like a peacock. She had no tail but she had something like a tail, that sparkled and flared. She made a noise rather like a peacock, too. But she still looked like a big monkey to him and she smelt good. He sensed she wasn't as strong as the males. He thought he would try to eat her. But only if the male two-legs wasn't there to put his hand on his neck and stop him.

But the big two-legs didn't go away. He stayed.

He took the cub out of the cage. The cub liked being held by the two-legs. It made him feel very safe. It was strange, smelling his food-smell and, at the same time, liking to be held close to him. The anger was still there because of what had been put on his feet. But he already knew better than to bite the male two-legs. The puzzling thing was that he no longer wanted to.

That day he learnt to play.

Of course, he had played before, with his brother. But not for a long time. Not during the bad time in the dark, rocking place. They had been too fearful and wretched. But now he remembered that it was good to chase something that rolled along the ground, to catch it and leap with it, knocking it into the air and batting it with his muffled paws. He almost forgot they were muffled.

The female two-legs made the peacock noise and the rain-on-leaves noise with her front feet. She crouched down and made the same sound over and over again: "Boots! Boots!" He sensed she wanted him to come to her, and he wanted to come. At first he was too timid, but then the male two-legs picked him up and put him down close to her. She smelt good and her paws when she touched him were knowing and cunning amid his fur, scratching and stroking in ways that made him squirm and lie on his back and rumble deep in his chest. He had a vague memory of the rough tongue and the warm flanks and the nipple that filled his mouth with sweet flowing power.

He hadn't forgotten his brother, either.

And his brother hadn't forgotten him.

The bigger, stronger cub was not frolicking with a tender, laughing female two-legs, being fed titbits of meat in a pleasant sunlit open place. He was in a dark, bad-smelling, closed-in place, under the ground.

He knew he was under the ground because he had been carried, in his cage, down a long flight of steps into dimness and coldness. He growled and snarled all the way and tried to reach through the bars to claw the bodies of those who carried him, but he couldn't. At last he was released from the cage. The front of it was raised by some invisible agency and he came out with one bound – only to find his way blocked by cold black stone. There was a clang behind him as bars came down.

His thoughts were all confusion, rage, frustration. His stomach churned and threw up bitterness into his mouth. He clawed the hard, stopping walls. It was useless.

At last he stopped. He put his front paws on to the wall and stretched his neck, but he couldn't see anything beyond.

He had never felt so alone in his life. He had never

been alone, till now. He whined miserably.

A coarse, loud voice shouted, "Quiet, you little brute, or I'll give you something to howl for!" The threat in it was unmistakable. The bigger cub urinated with fear, then found a corner, pressed himself tight to the cold wall, and lay down.

He didn't sleep. He was too nervous. He shivered and all his striped fur stood on end. There had been something in that voice that filled him with dread.

For several days no two-legs came near him. He could hear them, at a distance, shouting. His food was pushed between the bars at the front of his prison on the end of long poles, while the cub clawed and gnawed it. As the days passed he lost condition and became listless with misery.

Two days went by without any food. And then the teasing started.

The cub sensed something bad was going to happen when a two-legs came into the dark place and made sounds that were the same as the shouting from afar. Unlike his brother, this cub had never had kindness from a two-legs, and all he knew of them was that they were the all-powerful source of food, and fear.

This two-legs, very big and very threatening, stood

over him as he lay in the corner he had chosen as a sleeping place. The cub didn't know the nature of the threat but he knew he was afraid and helpless. He held himself alert as he lay with his head on his forepaws.

"Get up, you," growled the two-legs. And it was a growl, deep in his throat, the sort of growl tigers make. It was almost the language the cub understood. The words meant nothing but the threat was clear. He didn't move.

The man prodded him sharply with something he carried.

The cub lifted his head and snapped at the thing that had hurt him. But it wasn't there any more.

"Get up," the two-legs growled again.

When the cub still didn't move, the two-legs jabbed him again. This time the sharp thing nearly pierced his hide. He jumped up with a snarl of pain and swiped at the thing with his claws. It went away, came back, jabbed again, was snatched away before the cub could seize it.

The cub was infuriated. He crouched, ready to spring at his tormentor. But he couldn't, because a volley of small jabs kept him at bay.

"Come on, you little pig's whelp, you miserable mangy little runt! Spring at me! Just try it! You'll never make the arena, you weakling! Come on, coward, what are you waiting for?" The threatening voice went on and on, daring him, ordering him, provoking him, rousing him for battle – but always keeping him off, prodding him back. At last the cub, infuriated beyond bearing, did leap, full at the sharpened stick, not even seeing it in his blind rage. It didn't pierce him. It vanished, as the man leapt aside and the cub dropped to the ground.

"Good," said the two-legs. "Good. Now you're learning."

He gave him a piece of meat and went away.

So. That was it. He was supposed to spring. If he sprang, the sharp thing would not hurt him. It would only hurt and torment him if he did not spring. If he sprang, he would get meat.

Thus the little tiger began to absorb the lessons that prepared him for his destiny.

Aurelia's mother and father came to visit her several days after Boots's first appearance.

It was unusual for the Emperor and Empress to visit their daughter together. The Emperor was an intensely busy man and had all too little time for his youngest child (Aurelia had two older brothers, already away in the army). But that didn't mean he was not devoted to her. Aurelia was the decoration on his life, his sweet reward after the essential sons, both troublesome and hard to love. He was conscious of his duty towards her now she was nearing womanhood, but left the details to his wife.

Except that now he had sent his child a daring and extraordinary present, which his wife fiercely opposed.

"Are you mad, Septimus?" she had railed. "A wild animal! Supposing it hurts her!"

"I have given orders. It won't hurt her."

"But why? Why take the slightest risk?"

She'd stood before him, her fists clenched, her face pale. This youngest child was the dearest of all to her, after two sons whom she had never been allowed to be close to. The Emperor drew her down beside him and unlocked her fingers.

"Our daughter is as much the child of Caesar as her brothers. She too must be brave and proud. Would you have her play tamely with caged birds and goldfish for ever? She must show her mettle. She'll teach the tiger to be gentle, and he will teach her to be strong."

She stared at him. She knew what was in his mind. He was already imagining Aurelia going about the city in her carriage with a *tiger* at her side, her hand on its head, the people gazing at her in awe. "See! Caesar's daughter rides with a tiger and is not afraid!"

For several days Caesar had let his thoughts stray to Aurelia more than usual. How had she received his gift? It was even possible that she might reject it. She had a will of her own. Besides, many young girls would be afraid of having a wild beast for a pet. He needed to know that his daughter had responded to the challenge as he wished her to.

When he heard that she had objected to the drawing of the animal's claws, he tasted uncertainty, even alarm. But the animal-keeper had the solution. Leather pouches that would enclose the cub's feet and keep his child safe. Better! Much better. He sent a purse of coins to the slave as a reward for his initiative.

Now he stayed away from the Senate for an hour to accompany his wife on her regular morning visit to their daughter and her new companion. They were accompanied by a middle-aged woman who had been Aurelia's nurse when she was younger, and who now lived in retirement in the palace and assumed privileges that no one had given her. She was entirely on the Empress's side.

"It's not right, Your Honour, not right at all! How can it be right to give a young girl a wild beast as a pet?

The gods made wild animals to be *rugs* and *wall hangings*, not playmates!"

Caesar didn't bother answering her. The woman had been a palace fixture since she'd been engaged as a wet nurse when Aurelia was born, and she had been interfering and even criticising ever since. He hardly heard her prattle any more. He was looking eagerly ahead of him as they entered the courtyard.

There they were, already frolicking together. The cub in his leather protectors was crouched in the sunlight, his striped fur glowing boldly, his head on his stretched-out front paws, his hind quarters raised and shifting to and fro, watching intently while the girl drew a string with a tuft of cloth on its end across the floor. His haunches quivered twice – then he pounced. She jerked the lure away just in time. The cub crouched, quivered, pounced again, and this time he got his muffled front paws on the thing and a moment later, had bitten it off its string and was flinging it in the air.

A young man stood in the shadow of an overhanging roof. His eyes never left the cub.

"Who is that boy?" asked the nurse.

"The keeper, of course."

"Did Your Honour give permission for him to be alone with my young lady?" she asked sharply.

"Yes, yes," he said irritably. "Why not? She must have someone with her until we are sure the creature is tame. In any case, all her servants are close at hand."

This wasn't entirely true. Aurelia's personal staff – chiefly female – were in hiding. *They* were frightened of Boots, even if Aurelia wasn't. In the event of a mishap they would have been quite useless. The Empress, suddenly alerted by the nurse's questions, guessed that.

"I want there to be guards. Not just that boy. Older men, with weapons."

He hesitated. He was watching with satisfaction and pride the fearless way the princess was now chasing the cub, trying to wrest the toy back from him. She held it boldly in both hands, close to his mouth, and tugged it while the cub growled playfully and braced his big, covered feet.

"Whatever you wish, my love. Give what orders you think fit. Of course we should take no chances."

"Of any sort," murmured the nurse, her eyes on the young keeper's well-muscled torso and handsome, bronzed face.

Caesar walked out of the shadows into the sunlight. Aurelia saw him and ran to him. The moment her back was turned to the cub he began to stalk her. The young keeper instantly leapt forward to put his hand restrainingly on the cub's neck.

"Pata! Thank you! He is wonderful. I love him so much!"

"And you're not afraid of him?"

"Not a bit!" She turned in his arms. "Oh, do look at him, how sweet he is! And I've named him Boots. What do you think of that?"

He laughed. "An excellent choice," he said.

The nurse sniffed and folded her arms. "Silly name for a tiger," she muttered.

"Oh, Nurse, don't be against him! Come and stroke him!"

"I will not. *I* am not foolish, whatever others may be," she said.

"Caesar, may I speak?" said the keeper, after bowing.

"Yes, what is it?" asked the Emperor.

"He needs a collar."

"Oh yes!" cried Aurelia. "A beautiful one, with jewels on it! And I need a lead for him, too!"

"Well thought of." Caesar clapped his hands, and at once one of his own slaves, who always attended him, ran forward.

"A collar for my daughter's tiger. Bejewelled, as she said. Order it from the leather shop. A leash, too. Tooled with gold leaf." He hugged Aurelia tightly. He couldn't restrain his pride in the success of his gift, at her courageous receiving of it.

The Empress watched the scene, narrow-eyed, anxious. The tiger cub already looked large and menacing in her eyes. She still thought the whole thing was folly of the worst kind. She exchanged glances of anxiety with the nurse.

But apart from engaging guards, there was nothing she could do.

CHAPTER FOUR

Visits

"**B**oots! Yes, that silly name just suits him. He's not a tiger, not him! He's a pussycat. Here, puss puss puss! Here, tiggy-wiggy-woggy, come and play pussy games with Relia!"

Aurelia's eyes narrowed dangerously.

She was entertaining – most unwillingly – a "friend", except that he wasn't, he was a stupid little bore and a maddening nuisance. His name was Marcus and he was her ten-year-old cousin.

"Don't tease him," she ordered sharply, as the cub showed signs of being about to investigate Marcus's wriggling fingers, pretending to be a large spider scuttling on the floor.

"I will tease him, and you too," said Marcus. "What've you done to him? Call that a wild animal? He's about as fierce as one of your silly birds. Tweet-tweet, Bootsie, come to Pata!" The cub obligingly pounced on the "spider" and sank his teeth into it. But carefully. He knew better by now than to bite seriously. One or two hard bites, in the early days, had resulted in sharp blows on the head and scoldings from his keeper.

Still, even a gentle bite from a tiger cub is not nothing. Marcus let out a yell and snatched his hand out of the cub's mouth.

Aurelia grinned broadly. "I hope that'll teach you a lesson, you nasty little tease," she said unfeelingly as he sucked his hand. Seeing him fighting tears, she relented and went to look, taking his hand in hers and examining the indentations that were rapidly turning into bruises. "Ffff! Poor old you. Does it hurt?"

"He ought to be whipped," said Marcus sullenly, more humiliated than hurt.

She dropped his hand. "Oh, pooh. It's nothing much. He bites me all the time when we're playing. Look!" She showed some little regular bruises on her forearm where Boots had been playing a bit more roughly than usual.

"I heard he'd had all his teeth taken out."

"Only his fangs."

"Hah! Lost his fangs, eh? How can a tiger be a tiger without fangs?"

"Well, you're lucky, he might have bitten your hand right off and run away with it, if he'd had them!" retorted Aurelia, sitting down on the ground and calling the cub to her. He crawled to her on his belly and lay with his head in her lap while she petted and soothed him. His tail twitched gently. "Look," she said, "he's saying 'I love being with you.' I can understand nearly everything he tells me now!"

Marcus watched her, full of envy. Though he would have died rather than admit it, he was a bit afraid of the tiger. He had to stop her knowing that.

"Let's play circus with him!" he said.

"No."

"Why not? All you ever do is kiss and pet him!"

"That's not true. I play with him."

"But not real games, only silly kitten-games. We should pretend he's a wild beast in the arena, pitted against a gladiator—"

"That would be you, no doubt," said Aurelia sarcastically.

"Yes it would! I know how to fight like a gladiator,

with a net and trident, or a sword – my father's not like yours, refusing to take you to the circus, mine takes me quite often! Here, you, lend me your sword!" he said suddenly to the young keeper, who had a short sword in his belt.

Julius's hand flew to it instinctively.

"I'm sorry, Master Marcus, but my sword never leaves me. Besides, it's sharp. You might hurt someone with it."

Marcus faced him boldly. His rank was so far above Julius's that he felt unassailably superior to him.

"Do as you're told," he shouted, "or I'll have you flogged!"

Julius looked over the boy's shoulder at Aurelia. Aurelia was watching, but she didn't intervene.

"I have no leave from the Emperor to give you my sword. It's not a plaything."

The boy flushed crimson with rage. He flung himself on to Julius and began trying to wrest the sword from his belt. Julius was in a quandary. He held the furious boy away, but he was frightened of what the consequences might be of defying a direct order from the son of a senator, let alone manhandling him.

"Princess!" he pleaded.

Aurelia put the cub aside and stood up. She stepped

up to the struggling pair and seized Marcus by the hair. One strong jerk backwards and the fight was over. She flung him to the ground, then went back to her place, sat down on the marble floor and began to stroke the cub again as if nothing had happened.

"You stupid squittering girl-pig, you hurt my head!" Marcus shouted, sprawling.

"Mind your language," she said calmly. "Your foul mouth will get you into trouble."

That silenced him. The hint was enough. He had a bad temper and he had been thwarted, but as he lay there he gulped when he thought how lucky it was for him he had not said what he might have said in the heat of the moment; for example, that she was the *daughter* of a pig. You might say that to anybody else during a quarrel, but not her.

After a short while he got up, rubbing the back of his head, and moved towards her. She smiled to him as a sign of truce.

"I don't want him to be a fighting tiger, even in fun," she said. "Come on, let's play ball with him. I'll throw and you can race him for it. You'd better let him win," she added with a little smile.

She'd had Boots for two months. He had grown. He was

quite a size now, but he had learnt many lessons, and he was so little danger to her that the heavily armed guards that had been engaged to stand by whenever the cub "came to visit" had been dismissed. They were expensive. The Emperor had overruled his wife after watching Aurelia and Boots at play on several occasions.

"The beast is quite safe. He loves her, you can see it. He wouldn't hurt her – she has tamed him with her strong will and kind hands."

The Empress was not so sure. "Does he really *love* her?" she asked Julius, who still accompanied the cub whenever he was at the palace.

"No, Empress. Not as we understand the word. But he knows her, and she has gentled him, that's true, and I don't think he poses any danger to her – as long as I'm here." He stressed this in part because he sensed that she was uneasy about his frequently being alone with the princess and would have liked to dispense with his services, and Julius was quite determined she should not.

"But he's getting so big! Surely large male animals become dangerous as they grow?"

"Usually, yes. But this one seems to be the exception."

Through delicacy, he forbore to tell her that Boots

was no longer exactly male. A further operation had been performed on him at the Emperor's command that had had a distinctly calming effect.

After this had taken place, there had been no visits to the palace for several days while the cub recovered. (Julius told Aurelia the cub had a mild illness.) Of course Boots had no idea what had happened to him, how he had been altered – diminished. The fangs, the paw-mufflers – these had been nothing compared to what had been done to him now. But apart from the swiftly fading pain, and a certain lassitude which was new to him, he felt no different. He didn't know he would never sire cubs, never have the ferocity and energy that he was born to. To Julius, who had a genuine feeling for animals, it seemed a pity in a way. But he knew Boots's destiny was a happy one, compared to his brother.

In thinking about this comparison, Julius became curious to see what had become of Boots's twin.

One sultry afternoon, on his way home from the menagerie, he went to the Colosseum and bribed his way into the cellars where the wild beasts were kept. He passed down flights of stone steps into a foul-smelling dark warren of cave-like, cage-fronted compartments, directly under the arena.

This place fascinated and yet repelled him. Here were gathered animals that had been brought from all corners of the Roman Empire, and even beyond, to take part in Caesar's games and processions. There were so many creatures, of such strange and wondrous shapes; although the conditions they were kept in distressed him, Julius could never have enough of seeing them. Great bears, both brown and black, that rose threateningly on their hind quarters. Leopards, glaring at him with their angry yellow eyes. Lions, prowling their cages with hungry saliva dripping from their great jaws. Hyenas – stinking, ugly little beasts, not so impressive until you had seen them, working as a pack, pull a man down and rend him into fragments... and then eat the fragments. Elephants, whose huge feet could crush the life out of a man, whose trunk could pick him up, raise him high, and dash him to the ground. But it was seldom that these gentle giants lost their tempers and attacked.

But the tigers! The tigers were the best. The fiercest, the most fearless, the most beautiful.

Julius went to the circus (in the cheapest seats, close under the canopy where it was hottest) as often as he could and watched the shows. Some of what he saw disturbed him deeply, but he never showed it or spoke of it. To do so would have been to expose himself as a weakling. Even Roman women had little squeamishness about the blood-letting in the arena. After all, that was what the circus was all about – the power of the strong over the weak, the domination of man over nature, expressed in battle and bloodshed. It was the masculine principal in action, and women responded to that.

Julius puzzled himself sometimes. He could watch the gladiators and other slaves killing and being killed in fights, and cheer with the rest of the huge crowds. Why did it distress him so badly to see animals being killed?

Perhaps because they were innocent. Yes. However ferociously they fought, however cruelly they clawed or bit or crushed to death – humans and each other – there was an innocence in it. They were doing what nature meant them to do, or what their human masters had trained them for. How could you hate them? Julius had sometimes caught himself having the strange thought that even if (the gods forbid!) *he* were ever in the arena and about to be mauled to death by a lion or a bear, he might, in the midst of his prayers, spare one for the beast about to tear him to pieces.

When *they* were killed, as they frequently were, there was something shaming in it. It was pitiful – yes, pity and shame were what he felt – when they were slaughtered instead of fulfilling their own destiny as killers for food and status among their own kind.

Besides, they were so beautiful. In Julius's eyes, more beautiful than people. More beautiful, at least, than *most* people. He could think of one exception!

He stood now amid the cages in the cellars of the Colosseum, breathing in the rank stench and listening to the growls and shiftings and howlings of the beasts. He didn't know which way to go through the labyrinth of narrow dark passages, and a primitive fear was inevitable in this place, where every corner held a dealer in death. He called out tentatively, and a heavy-set middle-aged man with a grizzled beard, carrying a lantern, came out of one of the tunnels.

"Who are you shouting at – who are you?" he growled.

"I'm Julius Minimus, the princess's tiger keeper," said Julius. The man dropped his aggressive tone at once.

"Oh. I didn't know, did I."

"What's your name?"

"Caius Lucius. What can I do for you?"

"I wanted to see the tiger cub, the one that arrived about two months ago."

"Oh, him. He's not to be viewed. He's in training."

Julius knew the routine. A coin changed hands.

"One can always make exceptions for specialists," said Caius. "Follow me and don't get too near the cages."

Julius followed him through the maze of tunnels, glancing to left and right as the lantern lit the cages they passed. At one he stopped.

"What's that?"

"Camel," grunted Caius. "New consignment just in from Arabia. Never seen one before?" Julius, staring at the strange, humpbacked creature, shook his head. "They come from the desert," the man said. "Beasts of burden, there. We got dozens of them, fresh from the ships. Easy to tame. This one'll be showing tomorrow. You should come. Grazers aren't as popular as the wild beasts in themselves, but they show the carnivores off. We set the lions on them. They leap on their backs or tear their throats out. Drives the crowds wild."

Julius felt the pores opening along his arms and bile came into his mouth, but he said nothing and followed where the man led. The tunnels were perfectly dark except where the lamp threw moving shadows.

"You like the circus?" Caius grunted as they went.

Julius hesitated. "The fights can be good," he temporized.

"Of course, it's not like the old days. When the Colosseum was first built, you know, they could flood the whole arena. They had sea-battles with ships modelled on real ones."

"That must have been quite a spectacle."

"You know what else?" He chuckled. "They had crocodiles in the water. Made it more exciting when someone fell in!"

Julius said nothing.

"In some ways, though, it's better now. They have to keep thinking of ways to keep the people satisfied. All sorts of fancy tricks they got – well, you've seen 'em. Want to see the lifts?"

He took Julius down a passage to a cave-like room and held his lantern up. Julius saw a wooden winch attached to pulleys. There was a sort of platform near the ground with a cage on it.

"Takes three men to winch that up to the roof," said Caius. It was clear he took a pride in the technical side. "Beyond that, of course, there's the floor of the arena. See that trap door up there? Look, I'll show you." He turned another wheel and a square shape dropped down. The cave was abruptly flooded with sunlight from above. "The beast, whatever it is, is hauled up to the floor of the arena and released. Can't get back down, has to rush into the ring and then – look out whoever's in its way!" He turned the wheel back and the trap door creaked shut again. They resumed their walk through the darkness.

"Go to the palace a lot, then, do you?" asked the man, who seemed more friendly now.

"Oh yes, very often."

"Ever see anything of a serving woman called Bella?"

"I don't think so. Caesar has many servants, I don't know their names."

"She was the young lady's nurse when she was small. Still lives there, on pension, like."

"Oh! The nurse. Yes. I see her once in a while. She hates the tiger so she doesn't often come when I'm there."

"Good looker, eh?"

Julius was surprised. "Maybe once. She's old now."

"No older than me," Caius said gruffly. "Here's what you came for."

They turned a corner in the tunnel, and in front of him, as the man raised the lantern, Julius saw the brother of Boots.

He stopped and stared. Already there was a marked difference between the two. Boots had grown bigger, but also fatter – Aurelia loved to feed him and she gave him more than he really needed. This one was lean, strong, powerful – and taller when he stood up, as he now did, rising to his feet with slow, feline grace as Julius drew near.

"Careful. He's a mean one. If you go too close, he can—"

Without warning the tiger leapt against the bars. His mouth was open in a furious snarl, and his claws – no muffling here! Julius saw them, long, curved, sharp as knives – stretched themselves between the bars in a downward swipe. If either man had been standing against the cage his belly would have been ripped open.

Julius instinctively jumped back.

"Phew! He *is* fierce! Was he like this when he first came?"

"Well – we've helped his temper along a little," said the man with a smirk. "And we don't feed them more than just enough to keep them alive and active. He'll be ready for his first bout in the arena soon. By then he'll be so eager to vent his rage, and to make a good meal of someone, he'll give them their money's worth, take it from me!"

"Will... will he be killed in his turn?"

Caius shrugged. "Well, most of 'em. die in the end.

But he'll give a good account of himself first. I pity whoever's up against him!"

"You pity them?" Julius asked, startled.

The man glanced at him. "Manner of speaking," he said. "You can't afford pity in my job. They're all just slaves really, aren't they, animals and men alike – slaves, criminals, prisoners of war. It's all they're fit for, to entertain the crowds and glorify Caesar." He ran a stick across the bars of the cage, and the tiger glared and backed off, as if preparing to spring again. But he didn't. He growled and muttered and then lay down on his side, his eyes closed as if disdaining his tormentors.

"What's he called?" asked Julius, watching him, thinking what it might be like to be in the tiger's hide – in his head.

"What's he *called*?" repeated the man. "D'you think I've nothing better to do than give them all names? I call him Brute when I'm provoking him."

The tiger opened his eyes and lifted his great bicoloured head.

"Well look at that!" expostulated Caius. "I'll go to Tartarus if he don't know his name! Whoever saw the like!"

"He's intelligent then?"

"So it seems! The dogs and that, they're quite sharp,

you can train them to come to a whistle, do what you tell 'em. There was a dog here once – wild when he came, but I managed to teach him tricks. Got so he knew me... I tried to buy him, but I couldn't. Sorry when he went." He glanced overhead.

"And the elephants!" he went on after a moment. "Now there's a clever beast and no mistake. You can't help respecting the elephants, they know what's happening to them, and they know what's happening to their fellows, almost like us.

"Did you ever hear tell about a time – oh, centuries ago when Pompey was Emperor when he ordered a half-dozen elephants into the arena and set twenty starving lions on 'em? And when they were downed, and being eaten, but still alive, they lay there making such sounds, and put up their trunks as if they was beseeching pity, or a-saying of their death-prayers – that was one time the crowd didn't like it! They say that fifty thousand people rose to their feet as one man, and wept, and cursed Caesar, and shouted for the elephants to be spared – that *was* a sight to fill you with pity, if you like! But it was too late by then."

Julius swallowed hard. The pictures in his mind almost unmanned him.

"Is that the only time?"

"What?"

"That the crowd has been... on the side of the animals."

The man scratched his beard.

"The only time I've heard of. It was only because the elephants was so big and – and sorrowful, somehow." There was a long silence while they watched the tiger, each with his own thoughts. When he spoke again, Caius's voice was very quiet, as if he were afraid one of his fellows would hear him.

"It does go to your heart sometimes to see something so – so..."

"Magnificent..."

"Yes. Magnificent. When you see something so magnificent brought low, just to make the crowds happy."

"Doesn't it ever seem... wrong, to you?" Julius asked eagerly.

The man seemed to come back to himself. He gave Julius a look – whether of contempt or warning, he couldn't tell.

"You'd be no good around here! You'd best get back to your pampered house cat, and leave the circus to men who've put a callous on their feelings for the Emperor's sake. Go on about your business now, I've got work to do."

★

When the two-legs had gone, Brute sat up and began to groom himself.

He never did this when any two-legs were watching. He got such comfort and satisfaction out of licking and cleaning his fur that he had a sense of intrusion if he wasn't alone. He couldn't do it when he was filled with hatred and fury, only when he felt calm, and for this he needed to be by himself.

The rocky hole he lived in was to him like the worst nightmare of imprisonment would be to a human being. There was no natural light. The air was fetid; it brought him no more than a tantalising whiff of anything natural and good. He could smell only the reek of other unhappy, confined creatures, and sometimes – when the circus was in progress above him – terrifying sounds and the strong scent of blood, that nearly drove Brute mad. The smells were in every breath he drew, and smells are a tiger's language. The hate and fear of his fellow prisoners, the blood-letting and roars of the crowd above, had become part of him. They fed into his own rage and strengthened it.

He still missed his brother, but in a more unfocused way.

When he lay down to sleep on the hard stone floor,

he felt an absence, a vacancy where the other ought to be. He didn't visualise him or grieve for him. He just felt incomplete.

In the cage opposite him was an old bear.

It was not the bear he'd travelled with. This bear had been in the circus for a long time. He had appeared in the arena often, and was a favourite with the crowds, which explained why he was still alive. When he loped into the ring on all fours, or was led in on a chain on his hind legs, the crowd would roar their recognition, and throw bits of food to him which he was sometimes allowed to eat. His performance was to fight off dogs that were set to bait him. In the early days, he had had to fight desperately against a pack of them, but nowadays only a few dogs were set on him, and care was taken that he was not outmatched. He was nearly always able to throw himself back on his haunches, grasp the springing animals in his great arms and hug them to death one by one, keeping the others off with snapping teeth. But he never escaped without some bites. His thick brown fur was bald in places, where the scars had healed.

The bear was the only animal that Brute ever saw come back down from above. When he was injured, the tiger would scent the blood and yowl. It was mostly from the bear that he received his sense that when animals went *up there*, terrible things happened. He was afraid, and yet he waited his turn with something like eagerness.

He wanted to fight, rend and kill. And *up there*, his instincts told him, that was what happened.

Chapter Five

Marcus

The boy Marcus was plotting his revenge on Aurelia and her pet.

Not her pet tiger. Her pet *keeper*. That was how Marcus saw Julius, as Aurelia's tame man. Between them, the slave and his young mistress had cheated Marcus of his pleasure, humiliated him and hurled him to the ground. They had *brought him low*. He wasn't going to stand for *that*. Not him – what, a senator's son – swallow such an insult? No, no matter how high Aurelia set herself above him.

But he had to be careful.

"I hope you realise," Marcus's father frequently said

to him, "what a privilege it is that you're invited to the palace to be the Lady Aurelia's companion. It's not every senator who's close enough to the Emperor to gain such favours! And how is the noble girl? How is she getting on with that beast of hers?"

"She's all right and so is the 'beast' as you call him. He's not much of a beast, though."

"What do you mean? He's practically a full-grown tiger, I'm told!"

"Yes, but there's a bit of him that won't be growing with the rest, and that makes all the difference," retorted Marcus with a sneer.

It took a moment for his father to grasp his meaning. Then he smiled.

"And how do you know that?"

"I find out things."

"I suppose it's common gossip among the slaves that the animal had to be castrated. Well, and quite right too. The Emperor is too wise to take risks."

"I think it's like a lie to pretend she's tamed a tiger when all she's tamed is a sort of half-thing."

"I don't notice you objecting to riding your gelding," said his father. "I don't think you'd relish being put up on a stallion, not you, my boy, you're not enough of a rider. Yet," he added, as he saw the boy turn pale and realised he had been too scathing. "You're young. When you come into your full strength, I'll give you a more challenging mount."

That afternoon when Marcus went for his riding lesson he took a crop from the tack room and, when the riding master left the schooling ring for a moment, struck his horse, spurring it on and dragging on the reins at the same time so that the creature didn't know what was wanted of it and eventually reared him off. Marcus, who was not a coward, immediately remounted and rode round the ring at full gallop, lashing the horse all the way. The master reappeared, stood for a moment in astonishment, then sprang in front of the horse and grabbed the bridle, bringing it to such a sudden halt that Marcus came off again.

"What do you think you're doing?" the master asked furiously.

Marcus stood up, trying to control his breathing. "He's very high-spirited today," said the boy. "He threw me off before. He wanted the devil run out of him so I obliged him."

"Your horse is one of the quietest in the stables! Why were you using a crop on him? You know I forbid it! Give it to me at once, and don't lay hands on it again until I give permission."

Sullenly Marcus handed the crop over. "All right, the truth is I tried to beat a bit of life into him," he said. "I'm bored with him, he's no fun to ride. Why can't I ride one of the stallions?"

"Because your father thinks you'll be safer on a gelding, and so do I. Now remount and let me see a collected canter."

The hurt, the sting of humiliation, dug in a little deeper. They all treated him like a baby. He would show them. Or – no, not show them, not in an obvious way. That would be childish, and might get him into serious trouble. But he would do something to prove himself to himself, anyway.

Meanwhile his visits to the palace continued and he behaved impeccably. He chatted and played with Aurelia and Boots, but all the while he was dreaming great dreams.

He thought what fun it would be if Aurelia were suddenly attacked. Of course if that happened, Marcus would snatch Julius's sword – while Julius stood paralysed with horror – and kill the tiger with one stroke, and rescue her. Ah, then! Nobody would treat him like a baby then. He would be a hero and the Emperor would reward him. Marcus never doubted he was capable of such a feat.

His other dreams were all of the circus. And these he half shared with Aurelia, because, in this one way, he was her superior. He had been to the circus, and she had not. Her father refused to take her until she was fourteen. He said the spectacle, proud as he was of it, was not for children. What he really meant – and she knew it – was that he was afraid she would be distressed by it, and perhaps blame him for her distress. Or perhaps show by some signs that she was too weak-minded to enjoy or even endure it. She was far too tenderhearted for her father's liking.

But Marcus's father had no such thoughts.

There was an ever-increasing number of feast days in the Roman calendar. The people, never sated with sensation and the excitement of bloodshed, demanded more and more. And on every feast day, Marcus begged his father to take him to the circus. It was by far his favourite pastime. There was nothing about it that he didn't love.

"You could never imagine it without seeing it!" he told Aurelia. "Of course, I sit in the best seats, the ones kept for senators' families. If you came, you'd sit in the Emperor's box, but nobody else has such good seats. The excitement, before anything happens! It's almost the best part! I get goose flesh from the crowds, all jostling and shouting, getting really worked up before the show begins. I love looking at the arena. It's all covered with golden sand, fresh each time, as if nothing had ever happened before – raked and ready to soak up the blood."

She would shudder. But she didn't stop him. There was something horribly fascinating about his recital that she was powerless to escape from.

"I know where the trap doors are, by now," he went on. "You wouldn't guess if you didn't know, they rake the sand over the edges so the crowd will get a shock when some wild beast leaps out! Of course, they don't use the same trap doors each time. So I try to guess where they'll spring up from. And there are the big cage doors around the walls, at the sides. The gladiators and slaves and some of the animals come through those. There's always a parade first. Some of the animals that are tame, like the elephants and horses, and there's an old bear, too, are brought in and led round.

"Then the gladiators come in and march around the ring and salute the Emperor and the Empress, if they're there, and raise their fists to greet the crowd, and everyone shouts and cheers. You know what, Relia," he said, glowing with the excitement of the telling, "there's nothing as thrilling as looking at a man, all glittering in his armour, showing his bravery, and knowing that you may be going to see him killed, that in an hour or two he might be lying there dead. And he knows it, too. That's the strange thing."

Aurelia gazed at him.

"They must be very brave, those gladiators," she said once.

"Oh yes, they're brave enough," he'd replied. "They have to be, they're fighting for their lives, often against each other. What I sometimes think of is, what's happened before? I mean, not *right* before, but you know, I mean they live together while they're training, maybe they've made friends, and then there they are in the ring and they've got to try to kill each other."

"I wouldn't make friends with anyone if I might have to kill them," said Aurelia. "I'd keep myself all to myself and not even look at any of the others. I wouldn't possibly be able to fight someone anyway, but if I were a man and I had to, I couldn't do it if – if I liked them."

"Yes," said Marcus. "You're right. You'd have to think of them as your mortal enemies. You couldn't be friends with them."

"Do you think they ever have anything to do with the animals – you know, before they meet them in the circus?"

"What d'you mean, anything to do with them?"

"Well, they might get... fond of one, and then—"

"Oh, come on!" crowed Marcus. "You mean, make a pet of one, like you do with your Bootsie? Of course not! If they did, the animal wouldn't fight them. Think what a scandal that would be!"

"I think," said Aurelia slowly, "that that would be the most wonderful thing that had ever happened in the circus, since it began."

Boots was now an impressive sight. He was fully grown, sleek and plump and beautiful, and as tame and contented as any house cat. When Marcus (who longed to be tall, but never would be) stood beside him, the tiger came halfway up his side. He was confident enough now to put his arm across the striped back and tickle the thickly padded ribs, which Aurelia allowed. Boots would sometimes lean against the boy in a friendly way and then he had to brace his feet or the great weight of the tiger would almost push him over.

Marcus decided Aurelia was practically in love with the thing.

"Isn't he marvellous!" she kept *cooing*. "Isn't he the handsomest creature in the whole world?" She would crouch in front of the tiger and take his great whiskery face between her hands and kiss his nose and sometimes, when she fed him titbits, put her hand right into his mouth to show how tame he was. When he lay at full-length on the ground, Aurelia would sometimes sit astride him and dig her hands into the fur along his neck, kneading him to make him purr. Marcus smiled outwardly and sneered inwardly. If Boots were a *real* tiger!

"She who rides a tiger dare not dismount." Someone had said that in Marcus's hearing, and one day he repeated it to Aurelia.

She looked at him sharply to see if he were mocking her, more than just the little bit of teasing that she allowed.

"I can dare anything with my darling Boots," she said.

"Would you dare take his boots off?"

She started a little, and looked down at his sheathed feet. Larger pouches had been made for him as he grew. But they were still there. She hardly noticed them any more. But suddenly she saw them as a token that she didn't trust him.

"Of course I would! He would never hurt me!" she said.

"Go on, then. Off with them."

She turned and beckoned to Julius, standing, as ever, watchfully in the shadows.

"Julius! I want these foot covers taken off," she ordered.

"No, madam."

"What do you mean, no? I say yes! You don't mean you think he would claw me now that he's so tame and loving?"

Julius came and crouched at her side as she sat on the floor by the tiger.

"You think he has lost a tiger's nature?"

"Yes. No. I don't know. I just know I want him not to wear those things."

He looked at her for some time. Longer than he should have. She held his eyes with the steady look of command that she'd been born to.

"Very well, I must show you. Watch," he said.

He lay on his stomach facing Boots and began to growl softly in his throat, staring straight into the tiger's golden eyes.

The tiger stared back for a moment. Then he dropped his eyes, and backed away on his belly.

"You see? Even when you're saying bad things to him, he doesn't want to hurt you!" said Aurelia triumphantly.

But Julius just went on snarling softly, edging forwards after the retreating tiger, his eyes fastened to him, the growling getting louder. Suddenly Marcus and Aurelia heard something neither expected – an answering growl, an angry rumbling deep in Boots's chest. They saw his lips wrinkle and curl away from his teeth, which, even without his fangs, were still formidable. They saw the fur on his shoulders rise, his hindquarters begin to lift from the ground, and the tip of his long tail begin to twitch like a thing with its own life.

"Julius! Don't!"

But it was too late. Boots was remembering himself. Instinct, deeper than memory, taught him to recognise challenge and threat. Before Julius could jump upright and dominate the animal, the tiger had leapt on him and sunk his teeth into Julius's shoulder.

"*Boots!*" Aurelia tried to scream, but her voice came out in a squeak.

She was on her feet in an instant and, without a moment's hesitation, grabbed the jewelled collar and threw her full weight backwards.

The tiger and the man were writhing on the marble floor. Julius had his arms up against the tiger's throat. There was blood... Marcus sat as one paralysed.

"Marcus! Help me! Help me!"

He came to himself, jumped up, and grasped, not the collar, but Aurelia's waist. Together they dragged on Boots's throat till he felt his air cut off, felt himself choking.

He let go. Julius rolled over and over to get away from those teeth, leaving a trail of blood across the white marble. Aurelia clung to the collar with both small hands, terrified to let go. Marcus clung to *her*, his face hidden against her back.

"Julius! Are you all right?"

He sat up, clutching his shoulder. He shook his head sharply to clear it of the numbness of shock and pain, and then, glancing round, saw what was happening. In two seconds he was on his feet and at the tiger's side.

One touch, one masterful word from him in an upright position and Boots was cowed. He crouched down, fearful and subdued. Aurelia slowly unclenched her hands. The jewels that studded the leather collar were imprinted whitely in her palms.

Her eyes were on Julius, who was calmly applying the apron of antelope skin he wore over his tunic to his injured shoulder and pressing hard. Aurelia shakily clapped her hands to summon a serving maid.

"Fetch a surgeon at once," she said.

The girl looked at the blood on the floor and gasped. She was about to run on her errand, when Aurelia stopped her. Like a scene in a play, she had a sudden fore-image of what might happen.

"Wait. Come here." The girl crept a few steps closer. "I do *not* want my parents to know of this. Do you understand? When you fetch the surgeon, tell him he must tell no one."

The girl hesitated. It could cost her dearly to keep secrets from her master. Julius very well understood this, and dared to intervene.

"Princess, it will be better if you don't send for anyone. The wounds are not deep – see, the bleeding is stopping. I'll get it attended to by my mother, she has some skill in medicine." He raised his eyes to her face. "Believe me, if you want to keep the tiger, it will be better."

Aurelia was staring at Boots. She was seeing him as she had never seen him. Julius was right. He could be dangerous. Did she want to keep him? Did she?

"Go," she said to the girl. "Fetch no one. Say nothing. Bring water to wash the floor."

The girl vanished. Aurelia went close to Julius – closer than she had ever been. She could smell his skin, see the wounds on his shoulder up close. For a moment she felt them in her own flesh.

"Let me bind it for you till you get home," she said softly.

He was helpless to refuse her. She made him sit down on the rim of the pool, tore a strip from the loose part at the top of his tunic and clumsily but carefully tied it over the bite. He stared over her head, his teeth clenched, but not because of the pain. Her closeness was so distracting that he felt no pain at all. He felt the tickle of her hair under his chin as she worked. He smelt the scent of it and closed his eyes tightly. *Let me feel the pain! Any pain, but not this pain!* The thought forced itself through his fear-filled brain.

Marcus watched with narrowed eyes. He had once watched his mother attend to a bee sting on his father's neck. Just so had she bent over him, while his father sat very still, very aware, his mother tenderly and carefully pressing the sting out and asking if she were causing him more hurt... Marcus had grown up recognising the signs of love. He saw them now.

If Caesar had so much as an inkling of this! A raging tiger would be less dangerous then!

CHAPTER SIX

Aurelia to the Circus

Brute's time had come.

His trainer knew it, and told him, fairly glowing with a ferocious pride, as if he'd built the tiger – bones, sinews, fangs and claws – with his own hands. Brute understood nothing of the two-legs' mouth-noises, but he sensed the man's excitement and urgings and knew a change was coming. And the other animals in the dark, noisome caves under the ground sensed it. They sent their uneasy warning signals, especially the old bear, who had seen it all and knew when a fighting animal's time approached.

The signals should have made Brute fearful, but they

didn't. They set his fur on end – that prickly, alert, thrilling sensation, a good feeling – and made his tongue drip. He paced his cage vigorously, and even ignored the scraps of meat that were given to him to whet his appetite. He needed nothing to spur him on. He *wanted* to go up there, where instinct told him death awaited – not his own, but his natural enemies'. His will to pounce, to rend, bite and tear, was fully aroused, seasoned and seething for outlet.

As Aurelia's thirteenth birthday approached, Marcus had decided it was time his playmate lost her circus innocence.

He spoke to his father, who in turn ventured to speak to Caesar during an unusually informal moment when they were together at the baths. Both were naked but for towels and lying side by side on stone benches, pouring sweat caused by the heating beneath the floors, while slaves massaged their muscles and used scrapers to clean their skins.

"That impertinent youngster of mine thinks it's time your daughter was given the greatest experience in the known world," the senator mentioned, as the masseur pummelled him.

The Emperor didn't need to ask what that might be.

Everyone knew what the greatest treat in the world was. He grunted, turned his head away, and said nothing at first. The senator waited. Marcus had already given him hints that the reason Aurelia had never been to the circus was because her father feared she was too sensitive – not a quality appropriate to Caesar's daughter.

"He could be right," said the great man at last. "She is thirteen. No longer a child... She has to go sometime, or people will begin to wonder. It's her mother, of course. I'm afraid she may have put Aurelia off. The Empress actually has no feeling for the spectacle... But truly, it is a thing to be done sometime soon." He rolled his head to face the senator. "What would you say to a birthday outing next week – we two, and the two youngsters? Would it please young Marcus to sit in the Royal Box?"

The senator drew in his breath at the honour.

"He would like nothing better! Thank you."

"They are good friends, are they not?"

"My son considers the Lady Aurelia his closest friend. He deeply admires her."

Caesar said, only half jocularly, "In a respectful way, I hope."

"Great gods, of course! He talks of her in terms of

the deepest respect." This was somewhat remote from the truth — Marcus, in the privacy of his home, had often had to be rebuked for a spiteful tongue — but it was vitally important for the senator to put any thoughts of disrespect to rest.

Marcus was overjoyed by the news. Aurelia was not.

She took her reluctance to her mother.

"Mata, I don't want to go to the circus, but Pata says I am to go on my birthday, whether I want to or not!"

Her mother drew her into her lap. "What your father says, must be, *cara*," she said tenderly. "Oh, I know. You think the circus cruel. Well, just between us, so it is, but that is what keeps the people entertained."

Aurelia frowned. "I don't understand why all that fighting and killing should make people happy. It should make them disgusted!"

Her mother smiled. "It should, perhaps, but it doesn't. People are bloodthirsty. It's the nature of simple folk. Blood excites them and they love to be excited, it takes them out of their boring lives."

"But we are not simple folk! Why do people like us like the games? Pata loves the circus! It's not just because it's popular that he puts the spectacles on and goes to them, he likes them himself, I've heard him talking about what he's seen and he gloats just like Marcus about the killing."

Her mother looked about hastily and put her finger to her lips.

"Shhhh, *cara*! Don't criticise your father, or say belittling things about him! He is Caesar, and Caesar must not be questioned or spoken of disrespectfully! Your father shares in the people's tastes so that he will know how best to satisfy them."

Aurelia sighed deeply. "So, I must go?"

Her mother nodded. Then she bent her head to whisper in her daughter's ear.

"When it gets too ugly, just close your eyes," she said. "But don't turn away or cover your face. Appear to stare at the arena boldly. *Pretend* to look. Pull your *palla* forward to shield your face. You can shut a lot of the worst of it out like that."

"It's a pity we have no ear-lids," said Aurelia. "I'm sure the sounds must be as horrible as the sights, and I can't shut them out."

The day came, full of brilliant, hot sunshine like most Roman summer days. Marcus dressed carefully and presented himself to his father with his dark curly hair tamed with scented oil. He had told his body-slave to give him his first, very light shave, just his upper lip where the dark down had begun to gather. His father noticed at once and a mild word of mockery nearly escaped him, but he stifled it. He was pleased to see that the boy realised he had to make a special effort for this extraordinary occasion.

"Are you ready, my boy? Come, then – let's be off."

Aurelia took little extra trouble with her appearance. It was her mother who made her exchange her everyday *palla* for one newer and more luxuriant, and change her sandals to gold ones.

"Don't you realise every eye will be on you? You must be a credit to your father."

Ten minutes before they were due to leave, Aurelia slipped away to her courtyard to feed her fish, and while she was there, Julius arrived with Boots. He had heard it was her birthday, and had dared to bring her a small gift – nothing that would attract attention, just a small decorated box of sweetmeats.

"Oh, Julius!" cried Aurelia. "Thank you! I'm sorry, I forgot to send a message. I can't have Boots today. I'm going to the circus with my father."

Julius stared at her without speaking for a moment, and then turned to leave. On a sudden impulse, Aurelia touched his arm. She seldom touched him and the warmth of her small hand sent darts of steel through his blood. He turned.

"I don't want to go, Julius! They're making me go. I wish…"

"What do you wish, Princess?"

She hung her head. "I wish you were coming with us."

"Why do you wish that?" he asked in a low voice, after a moment when he wondered if he still had a voice.

"You're so experienced, and you know about the circus — about the animals — and… you could help me to — to get through it without crying and disgracing my father."

She looked up at him. His heart was pierced. To think of it — this tender creature with her love of even the lowest forms of life — fish, birds, butterflies — why, he had seen her carry a spider to safety when it strayed across the floor where it might be trodden on! How would she bear the sights that her father was forcing on her? When Julius saw her again tomorrow, what would he see in those sweet innocent eyes so urgently, appealingly looking up into his? What wouldn't he give to shield her from those wild bloody horrors!

But he was helpless.

Or was he?

"Madam," he said hesitantly. "Your wish – in so small a matter as my coming with you – might get your father's consent."

An eager smile spread over Aurelia's anxious face. She flashed away, and was gone for five minutes. This seemed a very long time to Julius, who used the time to dismiss the four slaves who were now needed to manhandle the large cage containing the full-grown tiger. "Never mind, my friend," he whispered to Boots as he was wheeled away. "Tomorrow you will see her." He firmly believed the tiger loved these visits as much as he did.

"He says yes, you can come!" Aurelia cried before she was even in sight of him. She flew up to him and panted, "He says you will be able to tell me the fine points of the acts, if he's too busy with his other guests. Oh, now I don't mind nearly so much that I have to go! You'll tell me when I must close my eyes!"

"Close your eyes?"

"Yes, yes! When it's going to get too ugly! Only you mustn't say anything. We need a signal. I know! You will give a little cough – like this!" She cleared her throat.

"Yes, I see," said Julius gravely.

CHAPTER SEVEN

"The Greatest Treat"

When the royal carriage reached the great Colosseum, the Praetorian Guard – Caesar's personal soldiers who accompanied him on every public appearance – formed a double line at the main entrance, and Caesar's party – including Marcus and his father, followed at a respectful distance by Julius – walked between them, acknowledging the applause of the crowd. It always made a spectacle special when the Emperor attended, but the people were delighted beyond measure to see that he had brought the Lady Aurelia with him this time.

"It's her first visit!" the crowd exclaimed among

themselves. "How lucky we came today! Imagine how excited she must be, to see the circus for the very first time!" Many were remembering their own first visits. There was a general feeling of privilege and rejoicing, as if the daughter of Caesar were passing through a sort of initiation into the glorious state of being a full Roman citizen.

Caesar glanced continually from side to side, nodding acknowledgment of the crowds, and Marcus, trying to imitate him, twisted his head, grinning with pride and excitement and almost bouncing as he walked. His behaviour seemed to shout, "Look at me, look at me, walking with Caesar!"

Aurelia, for her part, entered the Colosseum with calm, steady steps, her head, draped with a blue and silver *palla,* poised, the picture of youthful dignity. Julius, ten steps behind, kept the rich headscarf in sight and noticed that Aurelia's face never turned from the front. It was as if she despised the noisy crowds of common folk craning past the Praetorian Guards' leather-clad shoulders for a glimpse of her. But Julius had seen her at other times, out in her carriage, Boots at her side, waving and smiling to the admiring crowd, and knew that this apparent haughtiness hid a quaking heart.

In the Royal Box, under the merciful shade of the great canopy, Caesar arranged the seating. His place was dead centre, between Marcus's father and another privileged senator. He put Aurelia next to Marcus, and, with an imperious gesture, indicated the seat on her other side to Julius, who took it with a humble bow. Marcus was astonished and angry.

"What's *he* doing here, and seated next to you?" he demanded. "He's nothing but a slave!"

Aurelia tilted her chin proudly and replied out of the side of her mouth, "He's here because I asked for him to be, so mind your own business!"

"Well, I don't like it!"

She turned to face him.

"You've been *shaved*. You look absolutely *silly* with your top lip all bare. You think pretending you've got a moustache can make you a man like Julius? You're nothing but a stupid *boy*."

This unseemly conversation, luckily, couldn't be overheard because of the deafening roars of the vast crowd, which had begun as Caesar's party entered the box and didn't die down for long minutes. At last, when he considered he had received his due, Caesar rose and held up his arms. The cheering stopped as if cut off with a sword and complete silence fell all over the arena.

The Emperor gazed all around him slowly, so that each one of the thousands of spectators might imagine he was looking personally at them.

"Welcome, Romans. Let the performance begin," he said in a voice that, through long practice, and the wonderful acoustics of the place, carried without shouting to the farthest benches.

A blare of trumpets sounded, Aurelia clenched her hands in her lap, Marcus jiggled with excitement, and the show began.

That day's programme opened, as usual, with a parade around the circus ring. The gladiators led it, and it was just as Marcus had described, only no words of his could have done justice to their dazzling splendour. Their glittering brass helmets and breastplates shone like pure gold, the short swords they brandished also caught the brassy sunshine with twinkles of light that flashed in the eyes of the crowd. Behind them came a parade of animals and lesser fighting men. The old bear was led in last on his chain. He was greeted with affectionate laughter and applause, and was prodded to rise to his hind feet and give something like a bow to acknowledge his public. Caesar smiled, and leant forward to speak to his daughter.

"No harm will come to that old fellow," he said jovially. "You may safely give your heart to him."

Julius was watching keenly. He knew from Caius, who had become a sort of friend, that there was to be something special today. A tiger – the rarest of wild beasts even in Rome, unknown in any provincial town – was to appear for the first time, and he knew this could only be his charge's twin, the one Caius had called Brute. This "novice" did not appear in the parade, of course. He would be kept as a special event, a sensation, probably late in the programme. It was hard not to do as Marcus did – look at the fighting men parading before them and wonder which of them was destined to face the ferocious beast in the ring before the show was over.

Now the gladiators and the animals, having circled the ring, lined up before Caesar's box, and the gladiators raised their swords and cried out in unison: "Hail, Caesar! We who are about to die, salute you!"

A shiver ran all the way down Aurelia's back and her breath stopped in her throat. *We who are about to die...* "Are they all going to die then?" she whispered to Julius.

"No, no! Of course not. It's just a form of words to honour Caesar. Gladiators are far too valuable to all be killed off at every performance. Many will win their bouts or get the thumbs up from Caesar so they can fight another day."

Aurelia knew about the thumbs up – and the thumbs down. It was something Marcus spoke of, and used, though it was daring, using this Caesarean signal in his games with the princess when he wanted to show off to her. Thumbs up meant a reprieve, a pause in the game, a sign of something well done. Thumbs down, in their play, meant almost anything too rude to say, but Aurelia knew what it meant *here*. It meant death.

Now she nodded wisely.

"Oh, that's good. I hope Pata will give the thumbs up to all of them!"

Julius said nothing. No circus had ever been held when *all* the fighting men survived – the crowd wouldn't be satisfied without a few killings. His stomach was beginning to churn. Aurelia, at his side, was now bright-eyed, caught up in the excitement. Perhaps, after all, she would not hate it. It was so easy to catch this… *sickness* of loving the circus. He had it himself, and the only difference between him and the crowd in all its cruel blood lust was that he knew it. He knew it was a sickness, that his fascination for it was unwholesome, even depraved. But it held him nonetheless. He didn't want this beautiful, pure, and secretly beloved girl at his side to catch it. Looking at her face, very wide-open-eyed and gazing at the gorgeous spectacle of men and beasts before her, he feared for her in a new way, and longed to snatch her up in his arms and carry her away before she caught the plague of cruelty, of the thrill of blood-letting.

But on that score, he need not have worried. The first fights and skirmishes put a swift end to any excitement and pleasure Aurelia might have felt.

Her mother's eye-shutting ploy came into play almost immediately. To launch the entertainment, two tall, splendid gladiators were set to fight, one armed with a sword and the other with a net and a trident – a fork with spiked tines and a long handle. They circled each other, with much crouching and thrusting, and the swordsman got in several swipes that just missed his opponent. But when he was enmeshed in the cunningly flung heavy net, and the brass spikes rang against his helmet and felled him, struggling and threshing, to the sand, after only a few minutes of battle, Caesar did not even bother to rise. He turned down his thumb lazily from his seat and the net-wielding fighter knelt beside the one on the ground and cut his throat with a short dagger.

Julius, caught up in events, forgot to cough. But Aurelia's eyes had shut automatically. She did not open them again until a slight pressure on the top of her arm told her that she might look again. The arena was cleared and the blood was being raked over by a small army of slaves.

Marcus had jumped to his feet at the climax of the fight, and now sank down again beside Aurelia. He grinned at her gleefully.

"Well? How did you like *that*?" he exclaimed triumphantly.

Aurelia turned to him as coolly as she could for the pounding of her heart.

"It went on too long."

"Too long? Rubbish! They hardly got started! That's why Caesar condemned the loser, for not fighting hard enough. If a gladiator gives a good account of himself and pleases the crowd, even if he falls, Caesar often spares him, but that one was just no good."

"I thought he fought very... bravely," said Aurelia. She turned her head to the front quickly because at the word *bravely* her eyes started to sting. He *had* fought bravely. It wasn't fair when the net reached so wide, and a sword's reach was so short – he didn't stand a chance. She had wanted the swordsman to win *because* it wasn't fair. And now he was dead. He was *dead*. Dead, like her fish lying belly up in the water. How could a brave, handsome young man be as dead as that?

She felt the beginnings of nausea in her stomach. But the afternoon's entertainment was only just starting.

The organisers of the show knew their business. No two following acts were the same, lest the crowd grow bored. The next was an animal act. It was the camels, six of them, that first paraded in stately fashion around the ring, led by keepers. They wore beautifully coloured woollen coverings over their humps, and headstalls with tassels of dark red, green and blue trailing almost to the ground. They held their strange heads up proudly, looking both exotic and somehow kindly.

"I've never seen those animals before!" said Aurelia to Julius. He told her their name and that they came from the deserts across the sea. He had learnt about them by now. "See their big foot pads? They don't sink into the sand and can go for many leagues without drinking. They store water in those humps. And they can be ridden."

"How clever our gods are, to make such useful creatures! They look so strong and peaceful. Their drivers must love them the way we love our horses!"

Julius looked at her. "Yes. You may hear me cough soon," he said.

Her face froze. "Oh, Julius!" she breathed. "They are

not going to be killed – are they? Please tell me they're not!"

"If it's your father's wish."

Aurelia stared at him for only a moment more. Then she turned, leant across Marcus and the senator, her hand clutching the rail in front of them, and cried out to her father: "Pata! Julius says those sweet lovely creatures are going to be killed if you wish it! You don't wish it, do you? You couldn't, they're so gentle and fine!"

Caesar's dark skin flushed darker still, and he scowled and looked away from her. He didn't deign to answer. Everyone in the Royal Box became quiet and attentive. This was something to gossip about later – the princess daring to question the Emperor.

Caesar was angry, though he chose not to show it. He hadn't expected Aurelia to show her girlish weakness by pleading like this, for any of the participants, but certainly not mere disposable animals. He was ashamed of her. She sensed his unspoken displeasure and fell back into her place, cowed, her hands limp at her sides, her mouth open.

Marcus found himself feeling sorry for her.

"Listen, Relia, don't get upset. The show's hardly started yet. There'll be lots of worse things than a few camels getting chewed up. Wait till the lions come on!" He dared to give her hand a quick squeeze as it lay on the seat between them. "Be brave! You'll soon get used to it." He dropped his voice more than ever, and whispered, "I didn't like it at first, either, but now I love it, and so will you."

Aurelia, staring down into the arena, her eyes half blind with tears, saw the men who had been leading the camels stop the procession and strip the rugs and bridles from their backs and heads. They withdrew from the ring, carrying the caparisons. There was a pause while the animals, left alone, stood or turned in circles uneasily. The crowd, sensing excitement to come, fell perfectly silent.

Suddenly there was a clang, and a pack of hyenas was let loose from one of the side gates. They came running in, their hideous heads low, snuffing the ground, and in a moment their leader let out a snarling squeal and leapt up on the nearest camel, sinking its teeth in its shaggy neck.

Aurelia kept her eyes screwed shut for a full ten minutes, gripping the seat beside her with both hands so that her father should not see their trembling. But she didn't drop her head or turn it away more than just a fraction so that if the Emperor should look at her, he would not see her eyes.

She had been right, though. The sounds were as frightful as the sights, not least the baying of the crowd around her. The smells were also bad – the sweat of unholy excitement, and of blood. Her imagination worked so vividly that the pictures she saw behind her eyelids seemed, after a long time, as bad as anything her eyes might see, so she opened them.

The full clearing-away operation was not quite complete. She saw the hyenas, bloody-mouthed, being driven back through the gate by a hoard of slaves armed with whips and spears. Only two of the camels were left alive. They were clearly in a state of terror, rearing up, their heads thrown back, uttering gurgling cries of fear. Men were recapturing them with ropes. The crowd, which had gone noisily wild during the butchery, were now sinking back, satisfied, with smiling faces, exchanging remarks with their neighbours.

Aurelia looked about her, dazed. *What's wrong with them?* she thought. *They really like it! They don't care that all those beautiful creatures have been hurt and killed!* She had a terrible, sick feeling that if this went on, and if she stayed here until it was over, she would never be able to feel the same about her fellow citizens again, and with this thought her mood slipped into one of abject dismay.

★

There followed several more man-to-man fights of different kinds, with different weapons. An armed gladiator was set on by four muscular unarmed men, who, by circling him and wrestling ferociously, managed to disarm him, but he had already killed one and wounded another, and Caesar was moved to spare him. The dead man was dragged out by the feet, leaving a long scrape in the sand. In another bout, two men armed only with short swords fought each other until one was laid low – whether dead or not, Aurelia couldn't tell. The winner received plaudits from the crowd and his life from Caesar's upturned thumb because the fight had lasted fully fifteen thrilling minutes.

There followed an interval, during which the sand in the arena was raked, and a large number of palm trees and other vegetation in containers was carried in and arranged to give the impression of a jungle.

"This is the big one!" exclaimed Marcus at her side. "You wait! It's the turn of the wild beasts. Now we'll really see something! Aren't you enjoying it?" he added, looking at her pale face and clenched hands.

"Oh yes, very much," she replied politely, like a child at a party, unlocking her tense fingers to adjust her *palla*. "I'm so pleased I came." He looked at her doubtfully for a minute, but sarcasm was lost on him and he believed her, and was a little disappointed. He had half hoped she would start screaming and swooning, so that he could show his manly superiority.

Eight or nine men dressed as hunters, armed with swords, staves and spears, emerged from the side gates and began prowling through the greenery, as if searching for game. Some had nets, and others pretended to dig traps, which were really the trap doors that opened from below. These "traps" were covered with sticks and leaves as if to disguise them, and the hunters lurked in the false undergrowth.

"Who are these men? Are they gladiators without their armour?" asked Aurelia.

"No, no," Julius said. "They're not valuable fighters at all, they're probably criminals, or captives taken in foreign wars." He looked at them with a professional eye. They were quite tall – and some were fair. "They're probably Britons or people from the far northern lands. Our army is always sending back such slaves, and the strongest of them end up in the circus, where if they're lucky and fight bravely they might earn their freedom."

"Could you?" she asked with a sudden quickening of interest. "Could you win your freedom in the arena, Julius?"

"No, Princess," he said. "I'm afraid I'm no fighter."

Again, a suspenseful hush fell on the thousands of spectators as they waited avidly to see what would happen.

Aurelia waited too. She kept her eyes open now. The mood of high tension around her affected her and put her on the edge of her seat. She couldn't help it – though with a sense of dread, she wanted to know what would happen as much as Marcus, who leant forward against the rail with his teeth clenched, breathing heavily in anticipation.

Julius was also leaning forward. He forgot his duty to cough. His eyes were fixed on a particular spot in the middle of the "jungle". He imagined the tiger standing on the mechanical lift that would hoist him close to the surface. Any second now—

And suddenly – so suddenly that the whole crowd of forty thousand people reacted at once and many leapt to their feet – from out of that very trap in the floor of the arena shot a tawny streak like a long flame. It appeared facing the Royal Box, so that its open, roaring mouth looked like a red wound with small, sharp, deadly bones glistening in it. Aurelia sat spellbound – paralysed, as this apparition, moving with incredible speed, lashed out seemingly in every direction at once, and in moments three of the "hunters" lay sprawled amid the false jungle. One had his stomach ripped open and its contents spilt on to the sand.

One of the women in the Royal Box screamed.

Julius forgot himself. He took Aurelia in his arms and pulled her face against him.

The tiger hadn't finished yet. As the "hunters", totally unnerved and terrified, tried to flee, he sprang after them and soon two more were dragged down, though they still tried desperately to crawl away. The disembowelled one was screaming... And the noises from the crowd were no longer wholeheartedly enthusiastic. There were more screams, and Julius saw that several women in the crowd nearby were fainting.

Meanwhile the slaughter in the arena went on. Brute was savaging every two-legs that he could reach.

Three or four hurled themselves at the barrier, twice the height of a man, which separated the arena from the audience, and tried to clamber up it. This made the crowd laugh. Several of the more heroic forcibly checked their flight, hid behind trees and hurled their spears at the tiger, but they were so unnerved by his furious assault that they missed their aim. A spear that whistled past him – reminding him of his trainer's proddings – simply enraged him more, so that he pursued the thrower in an avenging bound, and tore out his throat.

But after a few moments of frenzied whirling, pouncing, rending and clawing, his killing urge left him. He remembered his hunger, lay down – but warily – beside his first victim, and began to eat the man's entrails.

Marcus vomited over the rail.

Caesar rose to his feet. He was so hypnotised by the spectacle that (luckily for Julius, who was still clutching the princess to him) he glanced neither to left nor right, but only below at the tiger, surrounded by bloody carnage, devouring his prey. He held up his arm and gestured. Instantly, armoured keepers appeared (including Caius) and bore down on the tiger, who got up and faced them, snarling and roaring defiance. But there were too many of them. With outstretched nets, noise-making implements, shouts and sharp-pointed spears, they drove him back and back till he reached one of the iron gates, which was raised and then lowered swiftly behind him.

Immediately afterwards, the clearing-slaves rushed out from the side gates with grappling hooks and rakes and ropes, and began to clean up the scene. It took a lot longer than usual, and while it was going on a few members of the crowd began to leave. The show was not over – their favourite, the old bear, hadn't appeared yet – but some even of the tough-minded, bloodthirsty Romans had had enough.

Julius suddenly came to himself and let Aurelia go. She fell back in her seat, her eyes glazed. Marcus was slumped beside her, grey-faced. The upper lip he had so manfully ordered to be scraped that morning was now beaded with the sweat of nausea.

"Marcus!" gasped Aurelia faintly. "You hated it too! You were sick – I saw you!"

He couldn't deny it. He just closed his eyes and swallowed bile. His mouth felt disgusting and his stomach still heaved. After a moment, he turned to his father.

"I want to go home," he said.

The senator said nothing. He was disgusted with his son. Showing weakness in such a childish way – in the Emperor's presence! He'd never live it down.

"Please, Pata," begged Marcus. His voice went shrill. "I'm tired. I've had enough!"

"Be quiet, Marcus," ordered his father sternly. "Pull yourself together! We can't leave before the Emperor."

But Aurelia was under no such restraint.

"I'm tired, too," she said, standing up unsteadily.

"Pata, I'm going home. Julius will take me." She looked at Marcus's grey face and took pity on him. "I want Marcus to come with us."

Her father cast a disappointed glance at her. He was afraid the occasion had been spoilt by the excesses of that one beast. "The show is not over..." he began uncertainly.

"It is for me," she said, and before anyone could stop her, she slipped to the back of the box and out through the long covered passage to the exterior of the Colosseum, with Marcus and Julius in her wake. Suddenly she checked her steps and turning abruptly, ran back up into the box. She hurried to her father's side and bent to whisper in his ear.

"Pata! You won't punish the tiger, will you? I – I liked him, truly I did! He was magnificent!"

"You silly girl, do you think I'd have such a rare and valuable beast killed?" said her father testily. "Tigers are not like lions, of which we have plenty. There are only two in the whole of Rome, and one of them as you well know will never appear in the arena. That wonderful killing machine you saw today is unique." He turned his regal head and looked at her sternly. "If you had the least idea of the cost of catching and bringing that tiger here, you wouldn't trouble to plead for its life –

especially as it's just made a name for itself that will be round the city in hours. It's worth far more than the few slaves it kills."

Aurelia straightened up slowly, looking down at the arena where the corpses and the blood had finally been cleared away.

"Of course, Pata," she said in a flat voice. "I'm sorry. I didn't realise."

At that moment the old bear, the final act of the day, appeared through one of the side gates. Aurelia glanced unseeingly at the huge shambling animal, but she didn't wait to see it go through its weary tricks, restoring the old carefree spirit to the great audience. She returned home in the Emperor's open carriage with her cousin and the young keeper, and none of them spoke a word on the way, each occupied by their own thoughts.

CHAPTER EIGHT

The Trick

After that day, many things changed, but they changed inwardly. On the surface, life for Aurelia, Marcus, Julius and the two tigers went on very much as before – for the time being.

Aurelia showed her father the respect that was due to him. But her heart was turned from him. She no longer threw herself into his arms or called him Pata, affectionately. When she had to address him she called him Father. He noticed, but it was beneath his dignity to comment on it, and if he spoke about it to his wife she wasn't able (or willing) to give him any explanation. So he decided to put the change down to growing maturity in his daughter.

Julius's love for the princess grew day by day. Since he had held her in his arms he ached to hold her again. The little head he had pressed protectively to his chest had left an invisible imprint there that called insistently to be filled again. He knew this love was hopeless and very dangerous, and he tried to fight it, but it took possession of him until all he had strength for was to conceal it from everyone but himself.

Marcus hardly knew how to deal with the aftermath of that fateful day at the circus. He had proved himself, not a man, but a weakling, whose stomach couldn't stand the sight of some real carnage. *She* had not vomited. She had retained her dignity, had been cool and calm, had led the way out of the box, and, all the way back to Caesar's palace in the carriage, had sat erect, pale, but apparently in complete control. For weeks afterwards Marcus lacked the courage to visit the palace. He didn't know how to come to terms with what had happened. And his father was furious with him, too.

"You disgraced yourself," was all he said. But it was enough. Marcus was crushed. In the end the only way he found to deal with his personal disaster was to push it behind him and pretend it hadn't happened. He didn't want to visit the circus ever again. But it didn't help him to feel better that his father stopped taking him there.

And the tigers?

Brute was now a celebrity. Caesar had been quite right in predicting that his fame would quickly spread to all quarters of the city, and that the hope of seeing him "perform" would make sure there was not an empty seat in the Colosseum for months after his debut. But Brute was unaware that he'd done anything extraordinary. He had followed his instincts and his training and had killed as a tiger must kill when he is hungry and furious. That this orgy of killing was followed by praise and titbits from the two-legs made little impression. Brute's life was still hateful, still confined, still miserable and unnatural. He still craved what every wild beast knows is its true destiny – freedom to hunt and mate and conceal itself and live out its life amid the sounds and smells of the wild.

On the fairly rare occasions when he was allowed into the arena, Brute killed again – not perhaps with the spectacular ferocity of the first time, but from the point of view of the spectators, satisfactorily enough. He developed, as man-eaters will, a taste for human flesh, which added to his enthusiasm for the occasions when he was allowed to hunt down and eat two-legged prey, and maintained his growing reputation as the sanguinary star of the circus.

Only for Boots, nothing changed. His fortunate, pampered life continued. Cat-like, he was content with enough to eat, comfortable sleeping quarters, and the petting and affection of his mistress. He no longer missed his brother or the beautiful, savage world he had been bred in. If things had continued as they were, he might have lived out this placid, unnatural life until he died of old age.

But there were cataclysms up ahead for him – for all of them.

After about a month, Aurelia began to feel uneasy about Marcus not coming to the palace to be with her. Though she would never have admitted it, she began to miss him. There had been that moment, at the circus – disgraced in all eyes but hers – when she had warmed to him. Besides, she was lonely; she was allowed so few friends.

Her mother had noticed Marcus's absence too.

"Why doesn't Marcus come any more, *cara*?"

Aurelia shrugged, her eyes on the ground.

"Have you quarrelled?"

"No."

"Well? Oh, come along, Aurelia, something must have happened! He used to come all the time."

"I think... I think he's embarrassed."

"What about?"

"About – about what happened that day Father took me to the Colosseum." Her mother waited. "There was a tiger that killed... a lot of people, and Marcus got sick."

"Ah. That wretched tiger! It seems to be all anyone can talk about. Last night at Drusilla's party everyone was describing..." She rolled her eyes. "Too disgusting, I had to retire to the vomitorium. Poor boy, actually *seeing* it – who can wonder? But in front of his father, and yours... What a blow to his pride!" She brooded for a few moments. Then she said, "You know, *cara mia*, I think it might make a nice gesture if you went to visit *him*."

"Me visit him? But—"

"Yes, I know. It's irregular. You are socially above him and he should come to you. But there are times when those in high positions show nobility of spirit by stooping to those beneath them. Come, don't you think you could? He is your cousin, after all."

"He's a pest."

"That's not genteel, Aurelia," said her mother reprovingly. "Now, I want you to do this, and I will arrange it. But you needn't mention it to your father. He has such strong ideas about protocol." She rose to leave, but stopped. "Why do you call him Father now, instead of Pata?"

Aurelia was silent for a long minute. Then she said, "I don't feel to call him Pata any more."

Her mother stared at her. "Is this, too, something to do with your visit to the circus?"

Aurelia looked at the ground and nodded.

There was another long silence. Then her mother drew a deep breath, and became brisk. "I understand. But you'll get over it." She nearly added, *As I did*. But that would have been to admit too much. Her union with Caesar was not as perfect as she wished people to believe.

The visit was arranged discreetly, between the two mothers, who were sisters. Aurelia went along with it, on one condition.

"I want Boots to come with me."

"*Cara!* Is that kind? A tiger, after what happened? Might it not seem to Marcus that you are rubbing his nose in his humiliation?"

Aurelia was startled. "But Mata! Boots isn't a tiger like that other one!" She shuddered. "Marcus knows that. He likes Boots. He'll want to see him. And maybe – I mean, playing with Boots may help him to get over... what he saw."

Some more discreet negotiations passed between the mothers. Marcus's mother, after consideration, agreed with Aurelia.

"One doesn't want Marcus to develop an exaggerated, unmanly fear of wild animals," she said. "I think it might be good for him to play with that tame creature. Of course the keeper-boy must come too. I know he has complete control over the animal. For my part," she confided, "I'm terrified of the things. Did you hear, by the way, what happened at the circus last week? That ferocious animal ripped a man's arm right—" She saw her companion turn deathly pale. "Oh, my dear sister, I'm sorry, I shouldn't have mentioned it!"

Marcus was overjoyed when he was told that Aurelia was coming. He'd never entertained her at his house before and he had his own servants and slaves running around in circles, getting ready for the visit.

"Everything has to be perfect! Clean the floor again – I see a bird dropping! She may take that for a bad omen. Bring more cushions for the couches. And food, and drink. I want the best fruit juices and sweetmeats for her. And for the tiger, some delicious meat – quail – yes, good, he loves game birds." His mother had to intervene to put a brake on his stream of orders.

"Does the young lady make all this fuss when you visit her?"

"Mata! Of course not. She's Caesar's daughter! It's simply amazing, her coming here!"

"Of course it's a great honour. Nevertheless, enough is enough." She clapped her hands and dismissed the servants. "Now, Marcus, I want you not to be servile. No exaggerated humbleness. Behave to her just as usual. That's what she will want."

"Yes. All right. But Mata – why do you think she's coming?"

"She's missed you, I expect. You've been her closest friend."

"Me? I don't think so," he said, flattered but doubtful. "She always treats me like a big nuisance."

"That was when you were little," said his mother firmly. "You're growing up now – you're nearly eleven. You can expect to be more nearly her equal now. Just behave yourself properly and don't tease or make silly jokes. Be a man. She'll respect you for it."

She looked at her son critically, trying to detach herself and see him as others might. He was a handsome enough boy, with his curly black hair, strong teeth and lustrous eyes. Though he lacked height, he was beginning to fill out a little, around the shoulders. Was it remotely possible that one day...? There were only two years between them – well, two and a bit. That wasn't much. Many boys were pledged or even married in their early teens, and some, where the uniting of high-class families was at issue, to older girls. A match between the cousins was not entirely impossible. Her ambitious heart almost stopped beating as this notion occurred to her.

Both Aurelia and Marcus grew secretly excited and nervous as the day of the visit approached. Julius was ordered to ready himself and his charge. He realised the importance of the occasion, and, after doing his best with his own appearance, concentrated on brushing Boots's beautiful stripy coat (which the tiger loved), polishing his "boots" and even combing his whiskers. But there was one vital matter he overlooked.

He had long ago learnt to feed Boots at appropriate times so that there would be no "accidents" in front of the princess. This time, however, he miscalculated, so the first thing that happened after they arrived and Boots had been let out of his cage was that he squatted, there on the scrupulously washed and polished mosaic floor of Marcus's private apartment.

The two youngsters didn't know where to put themselves, and nor did Julius, at this embarrassing mishap. Boots scratched at the floor with his muffled front paws, as instinct directed. Then he straightened himself. Something in his manner – looking about him as if waiting confidently for applause for his performance – suddenly broke the nervous strain both host and guest were under. They glanced at each other and then exploded with laughter. Soon they were so beyond control that they collapsed on to two couches, shrieking and hiccupping and holding their noses. Julius had to turn his face away to control his own nervous laughter.

Slaves were summoned to clear away the mess and soon the youngsters were chatting and amusing themselves happily as if no break in visits had happened, and, more, as if they really were friends and not just enforced companions. Julius watched them, noting a difference in Marcus. He wasn't so childish. It was as if the incident at the circus, which had so shamed him, had brought him on in some subtle way.

When the collation was brought in and set out on a low table, Julius noticed how Marcus directed the slave to serve Aurelia her drink first, and how with his own hands he cut a small bunch of purple grapes from the big bunch, laid it on a gold plate and handed it to Aurelia. *He'll be popping them into her mouth next*, Julius thought furiously, and then was shocked at himself. What, was he on the verge of jealousy of this – this beardless boy?

Boots luxuriated in the company of his mistress and her friend, and enjoyed being made much of. It was too hot for any of them to play. The young people sat or lay on couches, like grown-ups, and talked. The tiger lay for much of the hot afternoon at full-length, with his back and front legs stretched out so that as much of him as possible could press against the cool stone floor, well aware that he was being admired and talked about. Every now and then he would yawn and stretch, get up, and go to sit with his great bicoloured head on Aurelia's lap. This was heavy for her, in all the heat, but she didn't push him away. She fondled his ears and put her face down on the top of his head, and after a while Marcus, encouraged by Aurelia, timidly stroked his back and offered him pieces of quail (at the extreme length of his arm). When the tiger accepted them, the great teeth closing near his fingers, Marcus steeled himself not to snatch his hand away.

His courage was coming back, and the hateful happening at the circus was fading. He began to feel extraordinarily happy. He behaved well and didn't once tease or say anything that might annoy Aurelia. When his mother glanced in once or twice, early on, to see that all was well, she was satisfied with her son.

Aurelia was too well fed and content to notice consciously that Marcus was different. But as the sun began to sink behind the red-tiled roof on the west side of the atrium, casting long shadows of the flowering vine that partly roofed the open space, she was aware of feeling a reluctance to leave.

Julius, as usual, sat in a shady corner. He didn't stay as alert as he normally did. There was no danger. He closed his eyes as a way of keeping them from gazing at Aurelia. He dozed, and allowed himself a foolish dream of her. It was a very hot afternoon.

Marcus kept glancing at him. He was not consciously planning mischief. He was glad enough not to have the keeper's eyes watching him all the time. But it was wrong that a slave should carelessly drop off to sleep when he was supposed to be on duty.

And also, Marcus didn't want the afternoon's happiness to end.

So when, reluctantly, Aurelia stood up and said it was probably time she went home, Marcus suddenly dropped his voice to a conspiratorial whisper.

"Don't go yet. Let's play a trick on Julius!" He pointed to him and mimed sleep.

"Oh, I don't think we should—"

"Shhh! Nothing bad! Just a joke, to teach him not to fall asleep when he's supposed to be guarding *you*."

"But what?"

"His job's to look after Boots, right? So let's pretend he's escaped!"

The words were out of his mouth before he realised what he was thinking.

Aurelia looked doubtfully at Julius. It was true enough. He shouldn't be asleep. She glanced through an archway that led to a patio still in full sunlight. There stood Boots's cage, and there were the four slaves who carried it – all fast asleep too, sitting on the floor with their backs against the bars. Annoyance at their laziness pricked her. No, but this was too much, it was wrong! She looked back at Marcus's eager face. Her own broke into a grin like his, her eyes brightened with excitement; her nod said, *Let's do it!*

Silently they rose to their feet. Boots was lying in the shadow of the table, his tail gently twitching – his whiskers, too, when a fly settled on them. Aurelia stooped and stroked his face. He opened his golden eyes lazily. She softly clicked her fingers. He rolled over and stood up. She whispered in his pricked ear, "Come, Boots. Good boy!" And put her hand on his collar.

Marcus's brain was now racing. This was fun – this was a lark! But how to carry it through? Where could Boots be hidden for the few minutes – well, say half an hour – that would be needed to throw Julius into a panic, before they triumphantly produced the missing tiger? But the answers were there, ready, as if he'd been planning this for a long time.

He ran ahead on tiptoe, turning over his shoulder to grin and beckon. Aurelia followed with Boots at her side. Neither, in their soft leather footwear, made the slightest sound. They went through an opposite archway and into a covered passage. This led to the servants' quarters at the back of the villa. Marcus's servants had had orders to make themselves scarce after they'd served the collation. There was no one about... no one who could have stopped what was about to happen.

Boots, as he felt the dimness close around him,

stopped and looked back once at the sleeping Julius. But Aurelia's hand was round his collar and he followed her as tamely as any dog into the unknown.

CHAPTER NINE

The Catastrophe

Aurelia's home was a magnificent palace right in the heart of the city. The senator's villa, much more modest, of course, but still spacious and luxurious, had been recently built, and was on the outskirts. Its terraces, all on one side, commanded a view of the white city of Rome spread out over its hills – one could see the Colosseum slightly to the right, the Appian Way, the great landmark of the Circus Maximus where the chariot races were run, the arch of triumph built for Ptolemy centuries ago when he returned from his historic successes in India. This was where the senator took his guests after dinner to watch the sun set over the glories of Roman architecture, every building telling a story of its heroic and triumphal past, its unique and astonishing present dominating the known world.

But behind the villa was raw, stony, scrub-covered countryside. There were no terraces here, because there was no vista – Romans saw no point in gazing at nature. The hill the villa was built on rose quite steeply behind it and all that could be seen from the back of the house was a few distant olive groves, clawed out of the hillside, and the hill itself, reaching up and casting a morning shadow over the whole edifice.

Marcus led Aurelia and Boots to the back of the villa where the servants lived and where there were many storerooms and cave-like vaults for storing wine, olive oil, smoked meats and other goods. One of these was reserved for the very finest wines, stored in amphorae, great earthenware jars with pointed bases, resting in metal stands. Marcus chose this one because it was the biggest and most nearly empty. He thought there was plenty of room here for the placid tiger to make himself comfortable on the cool brick floor.

Aurelia, when she saw it, wasn't so sure.

She looked around the dimly lit vault. The only light

that entered came through some slits up near the ceiling, at ground level – the storerooms were dug into the ground for greater coolness.

"Will he be all right in here?" she said anxiously. "How long are we going to leave him?"

"Of course he'll be all right! He'll just lie down and go to sleep. We'll be back for him very soon."

"Yes... I don't want Julius to get into any trouble."

"Of course he won't! We won't tell anyone, only him, that Boots has escaped."

"Shall we do that now?" Aurelia, who was not given to pranks, was beginning to feel some unease about this one.

"Yes, let's. I can't wait to see his face!"

They shut Boots in the wine vault, closing the door behind them, and walked back through the villa to Marcus's apartment.

Left alone, Boots took stock of this strange new place. He padded around the cold room, sniffing at things and smelling the odd smells, trying to understand where he was. He was not used to cold, dark places. There was something interesting hanging above his head. He stood on his back legs and reached for it with his front paws. If he had had the use of his claws he could have dragged it down easily, but with the leather foot covers it was not so simple. Eventually he managed it by leaping up, getting one paw over the top of the thing, and with his weight, snapping the twine that held it to the roof. It was a joint of smoked goat and he was soon gnawing at it – not very hungrily because he was still fairly full of quail. He ate a few mouthfuls and then continued his explorations.

He was thirsty now, and he could smell something like sour water. He nosed one of the jars. He pushed it – it tilted slightly and he heard the sound of liquid sloshing about in it. He put his head under the jar and pushed it upwards. It fell out of its stand with a crash.

The precious wine flooded out and spread its dark pool amid the broken shards of the earthenware pot. Boots leapt away in fright, shaking his ears against the loud echo of the crash.

Nothing else happened and he returned cautiously to see what the liquid was. He lapped up some of it. He didn't like it much but it was thirst-quenching so he drank more of it. He began to feel strange. He shook his head again, and went on lapping.

He was getting a taste for it when something new happened. The door opened and several two-legs came in.

The tiger looked up. They stopped dead in the entry. There was a pause. A breath of fresh air with some other interesting smells wafted in past them. It seemed a good idea to the tiger to follow these smells, and he left the pool of sour stuff and began to walk towards the entry.

The two-legs disappeared as if they had never stood there, leaving a trail of noises. By the time Boots emerged into the passage, they had gone.

The attractive smell he'd noticed had not been the smell of human flesh – he had no interest in that. No man-eater, he! It had been the piercing, compelling scents of the countryside outside the villa. He was very familiar with these, of course. As he travelled back and forth to visit his mistress he had often smelt them. But never, somehow, so keenly. They had never seemed so – available.

He looked along the passage, and saw, up some steps and through another open door, the side of the hill with the shadow of oncoming night on it. The strong evening odours of green things and living things were in his distended nostrils, drawing him towards them more powerfully than the smell of goat or wine.

He became aware that he was alone. That there were no bars. No two-legs to restrain him. No impediment at all. Nothing between him and that tantalising bouquet of aromas.

The smell of the natural world. The smell of freedom.

He hesitated no longer. He turned towards the opening, ran forward, took the steps in one spring, and when he reached the outer portal, bounded through it.

Meanwhile Aurelia and Marcus, blithely ignorant of what was happening, hurried back to the atrium, to find the former sleepers wide awake and one, at least, in a state close to panic.

Julius stood in the middle of the open space, his face drained of blood, his arms oddly stretched in front of him as if he had fallen asleep with Boots in his hands and awoken to find them empty.

"Where is he?" he cried. "Where's he gone?"

"I'm sorry, Julius," Marcus said in a voice full of concern. "I'm afraid he's escaped."

Julius looked as if he might fall over. Aurelia felt an impulse to rush to his side. Marcus could barely hide his glee.

"*Escaped!*" The catastrophe was so great that for several moments no other sound escaped the keeper. Then he choked out: "Where? How? How could he escape? Where did he go?"

Marcus looked at Aurelia. But she was speechless. He

had to think of something, and his tongue didn't fail him.

"I'm afraid we – we fell asleep in the sun and... he just – when we woke up – he just wasn't there. We looked for him," he added quickly. "That's where we've been. Looking for him all over the villa. I'm afraid – he may have got out."

"Got out?" Julius gasped. "You mean, he's out there somewhere – free?"

Marcus hung his head as if in shame and nodded.

Then a thing happened that shocked all of them, especially Aurelia. Julius broke down, fell to his knees and began to weep.

"I'm a dead man," he groaned. "Oh, my mother! Forgive me!"

Marcus looked at him in contempt. A grown man – crying like a baby! At least Marcus would never do *that* in front of anyone! He threw a glance of disgust at Aurelia, expecting her to echo it, but she was not looking at him. Instead she flung herself forward and clutched Julius's arm.

"No, Julius, don't! Get up, please, it's all right! He's not *really* lost, it was a joke, a *joke!*"

Julius, who had been beating his head and twisting from side to side in his anguish of mind, became perfectly still. After a moment he raised his tear-stained face and looked into Aurelia's eyes.

"What are you saying to me?" he whispered.

"I'm so sorry, Julius! It was very wrong of us. It was a trick, to – to punish you for falling asleep. We took him..." She looked over her shoulder at Marcus, who was scowling at her furiously. She longed to point to him, to say, "It was all *his* idea!" but she was too honest. She had agreed to it. She had shut a door on her imagination and played this cruel game. No one was more to blame than she.

"We took him into the house. We shut him in a storeroom. We can go and get him out right this minute! Please, Julius! It's all right! Oh, get up, please get up, and forgive me if you can!"

Julius got to his feet. He wiped his face. No healthy colour had returned to it. He was still in a state of shock – relief so strong can also drain the blood. She was still holding his arm. He moved back from her.

"Show me," he said out of a dry throat.

Marcus whirled, sat on one of the couches, and folded his arms. His mouth trembled. His joke had failed, Aurelia had gone over to the "enemy" and Marcus had, for the moment, returned to his spoilt, childish self. *He* wouldn't help. Let Aurelia do it. At the same time, a frightening thought came to him. What when his mother found out what he'd done? Abruptly, he felt close to tears himself.

Aurelia didn't look at him. She took Julius's hand and pulled him through the archway and down the maze of passages. She remembered the way. Her relief was almost as strong as his. It was close to joy. She could reprieve him from the cataclysm he thought had fallen on him. He wouldn't have to be afraid now, or be disgraced! He wasn't a "dead man" now!

They were halfway down the last passage when she stopped in her tracks. Her heart seemed to stop, too, but it hadn't, because a moment after the first horrible realisation, it began to beat against her chest like the drums announcing some ghastly scene of slaughter in the Colosseum. The door to the storeroom stood open, and, beyond it, there was another open door – through which she could see the open country behind the villa. Their jesting lie had turned into nightmare truth. Boots had really escaped. He had really gone.

As she stood there, breath-stopped and sick, she tried to tell herself she'd forgotten which door was the right one, but she knew it wasn't so, and just at that moment hideous confirmation came. Down the passage behind them ran two of the senator's servants. They panted up, white-faced, and began gibbering out their tale of terror.

"Princess! We both saw it, we saw it, we are not drunk, it's the truth! A tiger, a gigantic tiger, alive, in the wine vault – it came at us – what could we do, we ran – it was going to attack us..."

Aurelia stood dumb. It was Julius who spoke, in a calm, level tone. "All right, nothing happened to you. Why did you go into the vault?"

Aurelia turned to stare at him. In the wake of his own shock of despairing realisation, he was taking charge.

One of the servants blurted out, "We heard a crash. We opened the door to see what it was—"

"The jar with the master's finest wine – smashed—"

"The tiger did it—"

"It wasn't our fault—"

"And the rear door?" With a hand that only trembled slightly, Julius pointed. "How long has *that* been open?"

The two men froze. They looked at each other. Then one of them began to whine and plead, pawing at Julius's arm.

"We'd just stepped outside for a breath of air – don't betray us, friend, I beg you, it's as much as our lives are worth—"

Julius brushed the man aside and ran to the rear door. Aurelia watched him without breathing. He stood there, his arms braced against the frame, his head turning this way and that. Then he pushed himself away from the frame and began to run up the hill, his bare legs beneath his tunic pumping desperately. He was soon out of sight.

The two servants slunk away. What their fate would be, when everything was revealed to the senator, Aurelia didn't dare to think – she didn't *bother* to think. All she could think about was Boots, and what would happen to Julius. *Their fault*.

It was Marcus's fault and hers. But *they* wouldn't be punished – oh no. They were too precious, too important, too highborn and rich. The children of mighty men of Rome were never made to pay for their mistakes, for their follies. They wouldn't suffer for what they'd done, not if Boots were never caught, not if he ran wild and killed someone. Not if, valuable and rare as he was, *he* came to some harm.

In all her life, Aurelia had never felt such a weight of guilt. She sank down under it, as Julius had. She felt what he had felt – the awfulness of what a moment's inattention, thoughtlessness, stupidity had brought about, and its probable cost. She remembered his agonised cry, "I'm a dead man!" and his childlike plea to his mother to forgive him. His mother. Yes, she would pay, too, when her only son and support was dragged away in chains.

When Marcus got tired of sitting alone in the darkening atrium, and, growing uneasy when the others didn't come back, finally went after them, he found Aurelia lying on the cold stone floor of the passage, weeping inconsolably.

He stood beside her, taking in the empty vault, the smell of spilt wine, the chilly evening wind blowing in from the hillside beyond the open rear door. At last he bent down and pulled Aurelia up by the arm.

"Get up, Relia," he said in a hoarse voice. "Get up. You've got to go home now." He forgot the difference in their rank. They were just two frightened children now. He shook her impatiently. "Stop crying, it's no use, it's done now. They won't blame us, we'll just say what I told Julius, that we fell asleep and Boots disappeared."

Aurelia hung limp from his hand, still on the ground, sobbing. He got hold of her under the arms and hauled her unceremoniously to her feet.

"Listen! It wasn't our fault. It was Julius's. And the

slaves'. They should have been watching. They're the ones to blame, not us!"

Aurelia could hardly speak for choking sobs. "Of course we were… to blame. If we hadn't… taken him away… he'd never have left me… everything would be all right. Why didn't we *think*? Why didn't we *think what could happen*? It's our fault, Marcus! Of course it's our fault!"

"How in the name of all the gods could we guess someone would let him out? That there'd be two doors open? Even if it all comes out and we have to admit we played a joke, we can truthfully say we shut him in safely. It was sheer accident and because of some stupid ape of a servant that he got out! Oh, do stop your silly crying, Relia. Someone'll hear you." He looked over his shoulder anxiously. "We have to behave as if nothing important has happened. Come on!"

He pulled her along by the hand back to the atrium, now in twilight, and sat her down on the couch, told her to wipe her face, and when she had, he clapped his hands. After a longer wait than usual, a manservant came running. He brought a torch that threw flickering shadows around the darkening atrium. Aurelia shuddered and put her face in her hands, but Marcus pinched her arm hard to make her brace herself.

"The Lady Aurelia is leaving now," he said curtly. "Call her carriage."

It was sheer chance that Marcus's mother had not returned to her son's apartment an hour ago to say goodbye to Aurelia formally and make sure she got safely on her way. Some important guests had arrived unexpectedly, and she had had to entertain them in a remote part of the villa. When they finally left, she hurried to the atrium, hoping she was not too late, only to find it empty.

"Marcus!" she called.

There was no answer. She went into his bedroom. He wasn't there either. She sat down on one of the couches to wait.

Marcus, having seen Aurelia off in her carriage, with sharp, whispered orders to keep silent, was lingering outside in the dark, afraid, now he was alone, to return to the villa and face the situation. Several horse-drawn chariots clattered by over the cobbled road. The twinkling lamps of the city were coming on below the overlook where he stood. He gazed at them unseeingly, fighting against his conscience, against beginning to see the justice in what Aurelia had said. At last loneliness and creeping guilt drove him inside the walls of his home.

He met his mother coming out of his apartment. The lamps had been lit now and there was a deceptive normality about the big stone rooms with their colourful murals, animal-skin rugs, embroidered drapes and comfortable gilded furniture.

"There you are, Marcus! I was looking for you. Tell me all about the visit! How did it go?"

Evidently she had heard nothing. Of course, by now the whole staff knew, but none had had the courage to tell their mistress. Marcus drew several deep breaths, his mind coming out of its frightened torpor. She would have to hear, probably within the next few minutes. It would be better if she heard from his mouth – his version.

"Mata, I'm afraid something happened. Something... serious."

His mother's hand flew to her heart. *In our house!* she thought. "What? What happened? Something to do with Aurelia?"

"No. It was the tiger – Boots. He – he ran away."

She couldn't grasp it. "He ran away? How could he? What do you mean?"

Marcus was thinking furiously. He could at once put the blame on Julius, but that might rebound against him later. Better to take some small share of it from the beginning.

"Well, Aurelia and I, you know, we were talking, and we ate a lot, and... we got a bit sleepy... and Boots was asleep, as we thought, and..." His mother was staring at him. No. It wouldn't do. Since he was a young child he had hardly ever fallen asleep in the daytime, even when the house was in its afternoon silence... She wouldn't believe it – not with Aurelia to be entertained. Not that they had *both* fallen asleep! He drew a deep, shaky breath.

"Mata, I want to tell you the truth." Not the whole truth, but as near as he dared come. She waited, a look of deep anxiety on her face, her hand still pressed to her heart.

"This is what happened. We – that's to say, I mean, mainly it was me – we thought we'd take Boots for a bit of a walk around the servants' quarters."

His mother continued to stare at him. She knew him very well. He wanted to drop his eyes but he made them go on meeting his mother's. His brain was working frenziedly. She said, "Am I to understand you wanted to frighten the servants?"

He hadn't thought of that, but, yes, that was probably his best bet. Now he averted his eyes, and nodded shamefacedly.

"And where, pray, was the young keeper while you

were doing this very stupid and unmannerly thing?"

Ah. Now. To drop Julius into deep trouble, or not to? He had to decide on the instant. He didn't care two straws for Julius or what happened to him – on the contrary. So what decided him was not the memory of Julius's wretchedness, but of Aurelia's reaction to it. If Marcus betrayed Julius, Aurelia would never forgive him, and he definitely didn't want that to happen.

"Well, he had to leave us for a few minutes. You know."

"And the slaves who carry the cage?"

Marcus was completely indifferent to *their* fate. "Oh, they were fast asleep."

His mother's brow darkened. "Well? What happened?"

"We led Boots down the servants' passage and we were... looking for someone to—"

"Terrify the wits out of—"

"Mm, but there wasn't anybody, and suddenly the tiger must have smelt something in one of the storerooms. The door was open. He went in and before we could stop him he'd pushed against one of the wine jars and smashed it. That gave *us* a fright. So we tried to get him out of there but he just rushed past us and then there was this door open to the outside and before we could do anything, he was through it."

There was a long silence. Marcus's mother sank down on one of the couches. She beckoned him to come close to her, and the second he was within reach she seized him and forced him to sit facing her. She was very pale.

"Is that the whole story, Marcus? Is that the story I'm to tell your father? Because this is a disaster, you know that. That beast is loose somewhere and only the gods know what it'll do. I dread to think what Caesar's going to say when he finds out. As for Aurelia! She must be in a dreadful state, poor child, she loved that creature! So you'd better be quite certain of your facts, because you're going to be asked to repeat that story until you're sick of it. If there are any untruths in it, they'll be uncovered sooner or later."

Marcus felt a sudden wave of fear. His lies might not hold up. There might be something he'd missed. But he couldn't go back on it now.

"It's the truth, Mata! I swear by Jupiter!"

She looked him full in the face for another second. Then she stood up without another word and swept out of the room.

CHAPTER TEN

Freedom

A wild creature released or escaped from captivity will usually run as fast and far away from its prison as it can before stopping to rest and take stock. But Boots was no longer a wild creature. Since he was a cub he had not been free. He was tame now, not wild. And there is nothing much more helpless and pathetic than an animal that has always lived with man, and had all its needs taken care of, finding itself out in the open with no idea where to go or how to look after itself.

So, although he went bounding quite happily away from the senator's villa and spent half an hour strolling and rolling about in the scrub, sniffing the air with all its myriad enticing smells of food and freedom, by the time it was completely dark he was already bewildered and hungry and lost.

He made a few half-hearted forays after small creatures that crossed his path, but they easily evaded him. After a while he grew tired. He found a sheltered place under an overhanging rock, and lay down to sleep. For the first time for many long months, he felt a dim sense that something was missing. He shook his heavy head in the darkness. *Another* should be lying beside him. But that other was not there. He was quite alone.

If only Julius had not been too distraught to look at the ground for signs of footmarks, he might have found his charge quite quickly, and put his own agony to an end. But he simply ran blindly up the hill, stared wildly around him at the broken landscape, and, not seeing the tiger immediately, ran off in the wrong direction. By the time he came to his senses, darkness had fallen and it was too late to do any sensible tracking.

What was he to do? He dared not go back to the menagerie where Boots was kept, without him. He dared not go home to face his mother – she would know at once that something life-changing had happened. So he found an olive tree and sat down on the inhospitable ground at its foot.

He believed his life was as good as over. In his despair, he thought his best course might well be to wedge his sword between two large stones and fall on it. It seemed to him that he had nothing to expect now but some terrible doom far worse than anything he could do to himself. Yet his gods argued against self-ending. They had given him life, and expected him to respect it and live it out to its natural end. But truthfully, it wasn't the gods or the thought of his mother's grief that kept his sword in his belt, and, after a long period when time seemed to have stopped, brought him to his feet with a kind of despairing resolve to face it out. It was the thought of Aurelia – of leaving Aurelia, never seeing her again. Of leaving her, moreover, with the memory of him as a coward.

So, to prove his courage, he took the most difficult option.

He could have gone to the menagerie first, and reported his loss. Instead, he stumbled through the stony darkness towards Caesar's palace.

How he would face the mighty Emperor and confess his dereliction of duty, he could not foresee. He only knew that it had to be done.

★

But Caesar already knew.

Aurelia had arrived home in a state that couldn't easily be hidden from her mother, who was waiting for her, as Marcus's had been, to hear all about the visit. To do Aurelia justice, she tried. She composed herself as well as she could during the journey back in the carriage. She was determined to say nothing, to betray nothing. But the moment her mother saw her, she knew something had happened.

"*Cara!* What is it? You're as pale as death! Did you and Marcus quarrel?"

All Aurelia's resolution collapsed. She fell crying into her mother's arms.

"We lost Boots! He ran away! He's gone, and Julius is going to be blamed for it! Oh, Mata! Please don't let anything happen to Julius!"

After that, events moved quickly. Aurelia was asked a few essential questions, was briefly soothed and handed over to her nurse, who was brusquely summoned from her peaceful retreat. The Empress hurried away. Aurelia was in despair. She had failed Julius. It was out of her hands now. But at least she hadn't said anything about him falling asleep. She, too, pretended he had merely left his post to answer a call of nature.

"Don't fret, precious! It's not so bad!" the nurse kept

repeating. "Why are you so concerned about that young scamp of a slave-boy? He should have been looking after you! And you couldn't help it if that nasty ungrateful beast ran away!"

She understood nothing. Nothing. Every kindly word made things worse. But Aurelia was now beyond tears. She went to bed and lay there, dry-eyed, numb and sleepless, thinking only of Julius. Once or twice, almost for relief, her thoughts strayed to her tiger. She thought of him out there in the night somewhere. At least he was free. Free? But no, that was no comfort. She knew he would be fearful, helpless and alone. But at least not in danger. No. Surely he would be caught. Perhaps if he were, Julius would be pardoned and it would all blow over...

She was too far away to hear the commotion when Julius reached the palace, entered by the servants' door at the rear, and asked to see the Emperor.

He was almost paralysed with fear when he was led into the great receiving hall and saw Caesar seated in majesty on a gilded throne-like chair. This was the most powerful man in the world, and, some said, the most ruthless and intolerant. He was generous to those who served him well – merciless to those who fell short, or disobeyed. He had entrusted his beloved daughter into Julius's care and Julius had failed in his trust. The valuable animal on which so much expense had been lavished had vanished. Absurdly, Julius remembered the collar. All those jewels... But Aurelia was the jewel beyond price that Julius had risked with his moment of forgetfulness.

"So. You have lost the tiger," said Caesar in a voice of iron.

Julius fell on his face.

"Before I tell you what I intend to do with you, a question. Stand up." Before Julius could move, the two slaves escorting him hauled him to his feet. "You understand animals. What will the tiger do?"

At first, Julius couldn't speak. But as he thought about this question, he found his voice, though it croaked and wobbled. "Caesar, I think he will do what a pet cat would do. Try to find his way home."

"Home? Do you mean, to the menagerie?"

Julius struggled with the wool of fear that was clogging his brain. "Perhaps. Or... he might try to come here."

"Could he find his way to this palace, through the streets of the city?"

"I don't think so, Caesar. There would be too many

confusing scents, and he would be seen and chased."

"If he is chased, will he attack?"

"I think, only if he's cornered. He's lost his natural ferocity. His claws are covered. If – if I could find him, I think he'd come quietly."

"He won't enjoy freedom?"

"He'll be hungry by now. He's never learnt to hunt. He can't hunt with his feet muffled. Perhaps he has lost the instinct. I think..."

"Well? Speak up, boy!"

"I think he'd be glad to be recaptured."

Suddenly the Emperor, who had kept his voice down till now, let out a roar of rage. "Is this some trick to postpone your punishment?"

Julius stood perfectly still, his knees melting under him.

"Answer me! For you will not escape what is due to you, whatever you do!"

"Caesar, I don't ask for mercy. Whatever you do to me, I deserve. But I would like to do what I can to right the wrong I've done. I'd like a chance to catch the tiger and restore him to the princess. She loves him."

The Emperor's stern face darkened like a thunder cloud covering Julius's sky.

"Do you imagine I will let her *play* with him after

this? Yes, you will find him if you can. That I will allow you, because I need you to do it. But when you have the beast back, he won't be trusted, any more than you." He seemed about to say something more, something Julius sensed would have terrible import for him. But he stopped himself, and gestured to the two slaves who had brought Julius in.

"Take him away and secure him. At first light, the search will begin."

It was to his wife alone that Caesar spoke the words he had had in his mind.

"This matter, of course, can only end one way. With the death of both of them. Probably the tiger will be killed in the hunt. If the slave can catch it alive, it can be put to death in the arena, for the entertainment of the people. The slave himself, of course," he added as an afterthought, "will die a more private death the moment his usefulness is at an end."

Aurelia's mother was horror-stricken.

"Septimus, how can you! Do you realise what this will mean to Aurelia?"

Caesar's eyes narrowed. "Mean to her? It will mean she has lost her pet tiger. That's all. She is Caesar's daughter. She must learn to sustain such trivial losses."

His wife stared at him wordlessly. An all but unthinkable thought crossed Caesar's mind for the first time.

"That *is* the only loss she would feel, I presume?"

The Empress recovered herself sharply. "Of course! Of course," she repeated, trying not to allow any note of panic to enter her voice. But it was a great effort to hide her shock. "I just don't want her to be unhappy. She's so fond of – of Boots."

Caesar peered into her eyes as if trying to read her soul.

"I'll get her another pet," he said at last. "Something less prone to cause trouble." He turned on his heel and walked away, leaving his wife standing with tightly closed eyes and absolute dread in her heart.

CHAPTER ELEVEN

Julius in Chains

Something not to be expected, the sort of intervention that, had Boots been a man, with some belief in the gods, he might have ascribed to divine power, happened as the first dawn light was creeping into the eastern sky over the sleeping city and the wild countryside around it.

A shepherd named Rufus, out early with his goats to let them crop the scanty grass while the dew was still on it, spotted a strange bright striped thing sticking out from under a rock and thought it was a snake. He crept up to it silently, raised his shepherd's staff and brought it down hard on Boots's tail.

The tiger awoke with a yowl and leapt up, hitting his

head on the projecting rock overhead. So he was in double distress when he emerged from under the rock and stood in all his angry might, looking around, baffled, for the cause of his pain. Rufus, when he saw the huge animal he had aroused, instead of running for his life simply stood motionless and stared with his mouth hanging open.

That he didn't do what any other man would have done was because he was not like other men. He was a simpleton from birth. But though his brain was dulled, or perhaps because of it, he had a strange affinity with dumb beasts. He had struck at the "snake" only because he was afraid it might kill one of his goats. For himself, he had no fear.

For a long moment, man and animal stared at each other. Boots's throbbing tail twitched, but he didn't spring at the shepherd. Why should he? He didn't associate him with his pain. He had never attacked a two-legs and this one didn't threaten him. He felt safe with it, and his greatest need just now was to feel safe. He approached Rufus slowly and when he reached him, he gazed up at him for a moment and then rubbed his great head and long, plump side heavily against the man's thigh.

Rufus let his hand open and the furry spine passed under it. When back turned into tail, he closed his hand loosely around it and let it flow through his fingers. When he felt the lump where he'd struck it, he made soothing sounds and stroked the sore place. Boots lay down on the stony ground, rolled on his back, and began to utter rumbling purrs. His unease and loneliness vanished. Here was a two-legs doing what, in all his experience, two-legs did. They brought safety and comfort, and, sooner or later, food.

Rufus crouched beside him. He was staring at the leather foot covers. From them, his eyes, and then his caressing hands, roved to the animal's neck, where the earliest rays of the sun were bringing out the twinkle in the gold and jewels that embossed the leather collar half lost in the long tawny fur.

"Well," he said aloud. "Pretty things here. What Rufus finds, Rufus keeps." He laughed his strange, simpleton's laugh, and set about discovering how the five pieces of leather came undone. Thick in his head he might be, but his hands were cunning. By the time he stood up and made off with his goats, Boots was free – freer than he had ever been since he played at his brother's side in his native jungle.

By the time the sun was well up above the silver-green hills surrounding the silver-white city, Julius, accompanied by a small party of skilled hunters and two guards to prevent his escape, was tracking the tiger through the scrub behind the senator's villa.

He was concentrating fiercely on the ground, and was quite unaware of Marcus watching him from a rear window.

Marcus, tired out, had slept through the night, but he had awoken at dawn with a stifled pain. He couldn't tell what part of him it came from; but it took only a couple of seconds, and several deep breaths that brought no relief, to recognise it as the pain of guilt.

His father had sent for him as soon as he'd eaten – or failed to eat – his breakfast, and interrogated him sternly for half an hour. Already his story was coming apart. Had he had his eye on the tiger all the time it was in the storeroom? Yes... But he hadn't said anything about a haunch of smoked goat that had been found on the floor, with several large bites taken out of it. How could he not have seen the tiger drag it down? Marcus couldn't explain.

How *exactly* had the tiger pushed over the amphora of wine? With his front feet, Marcus told him unsteadily. If that were so, the iron stand as well as the jar would have gone over, but the stand had been found upright. Marcus shrugged unhappily.

"But weren't you watching all the time? You must have had a shock when you saw the tiger going near my precious wine jar. You must have seen how it got broken." Marcus, pale and sweating, shook his head.

His father looked at him piercingly until he dropped his eyes.

"You may go for the moment, Marcus, but I shall want to see you again later."

In the doorway, Marcus stopped. "Has Boots been found, Pata?" he asked in a squeaky, urgent voice.

"When the beast is found, you'll be told," his father said.

There were other questions Marcus wanted to ask, but he didn't dare. There was something in his father's manner that frightened him more than open anger. A tension – something held in – that spoke louder than words about the seriousness of the situation.

Now the boy stood at his window and watched Julius and the other men. Julius led them, bent double, peering at the dry grasses and broken scrub, moving slowly, a terrible air of desperation about him. Marcus noticed a glint among the dull sunlit stones and bushes. To his horror, he saw it was a shackle fastened to Julius's leg. Now he could see that a thin chain led from it to the hands of the man closest behind him. Julius was a prisoner.

It's our fault, Marcus! Of course it's our fault!

Marcus's tutor came.

Today Marcus had no intention of learning, at least, not lessons. He wanted information, and with the story of the runaway tiger on the lips of everyone who had any connection with either Caesar's or the senator's households, it wasn't difficult for Marcus to find out more.

"It's said that Caesar is in a fearful rage," said the young tutor, eager to share his inside knowledge. "The tiger, when it's caught, will be sent to fight in the arena."

"But that tiger won't fight! He's tame."

"He'll be killed by the gladiators, then. And everyone concerned with letting him escape is to be punished."

"Oh? How?" asked Marcus as casually as he could. It was hard to control the breathlessness of his voice, even for those two syllables.

The tutor lowered his voice. "The four slaves who fell asleep by the cage have already been condemned. They'll be thrown to the wild beasts in next week's circus. As to the keeper, they're saying Caesar has something special in store for *him*. But only after he's caught the tiger."

Marcus jumped up, sat down, got up again. He was breathing hard, as if he'd been running a race.

"I can't study today," he said abruptly. "You're dismissed."

"But Master Marcus——"

"Do as you're told."

Bewildered, the young man stood up, bowed, and withdrew. Marcus stood with his head down, dripping sweat on the mosaic floor. Then he gasped. He had noticed with a terrible pang of fear that the drops were falling on a face, depicted in tiny pieces of coloured stone. It was the face of the goddess Minerva, who now appeared to be crying.

A fearful omen, surely! A goddess, weeping for him! Marcus fled to his bedroom and flung himself face down on the bed.

While Marcus lay trembling with fear and guilt, and Julius in chains tracked Boots into the hot, dry hinterland, Aurelia was in her mother's private apartment where she had been summoned. Her mother had decided it was better for her to learn the terrible news from her than from palace gossip.

"My own darling child," she began tenderly, drawing Aurelia close to her. "I have something to tell you that I'm afraid will upset you very much. But you must be brave. The gods have decreed that we must all suffer sorrow and losses in this life. No one escapes. What matters is how we face our lot."

Aurelia drew back, and stared at her mother with eyes enormous with fear.

"Oh, Mata, he's not dead, is he?" she gasped.

Her mother pulled her swiftly forward, muffling her mouth against her breast.

"Hush, *cara*! Don't!" she whispered frantically. For she knew, with a mother's instinctive knowledge, that it was not the tiger she meant.

Aurelia wrenched herself free. "Is he dead? Tell me yes or no!"

Her mother shook her head. Aurelia turned faint from relief and her mother grasped her by the arms. "Listen, and accept. He lives, so far. I don't know how your father will punish him for his crime."

"Crime? What crime?"

"The law of Rome says it's a crime to fail in duty and obedience. Julius failed in his duty, and for that he must suffer punishment. No, my child, my sweet one, don't look like that. And don't think of begging for him to be spared. If your father had the least idea that you have forgotten — even for a moment, out of pity — that he is only a slave, *believe me* his fate would be far worse. There are — there are many ways a man can die. Until this misfortune, he served well. I think," she added, looking away from Aurelia's frantic eyes, "that if he can catch Boots, your father might spare his life. But don't hope too hard for it, and, in the name of all the gods together, Aurelia, don't even hint to your father that you—" She stopped.

"That I love him," Aurelia said with sudden steadiness.

Her mother gave a stifled scream at the words. Then she whirled to face the *larium* — the household shrine where statuettes of the hearth-protecting gods stood in a small wooden cupboard.

She dragged Aurelia to the ground and they both prayed their own private prayers. If their gods were listening, they might have been much confused by the wild difference in what was being asked of them.

"Oh, great ones!" prayed the mother, silently and frantically. "Shut your ears to her shame! She doesn't mean it. She's only a child! I have told her since she could understand simple words that we are not free to love whom we will!" Feeling Aurelia under her hand, trembling with emotion, she threw back her head. "Oh, gods, forgive me! Much of the blame is mine. I knew the moment I saw that young man that he might be dangerous for her. Bring her back to a proper sense of her position and her destiny, or what will become of us?"

"Oh, spirits of my ancestors," prayed the daughter, no less fervently. "He may be only a slave, but he is a man, a good man with a noble heart. Don't let my father have him killed! If that happens I shall not bear it!"

But although Aurelia was a pious girl, she feared she couldn't trust any of the household gods, or indeed great Jove himself, to save Julius. She must somehow do it herself.

CHAPTER TWELVE

Aurelia's Secret

Since his encounter with the shepherd, Boots's view of freedom had changed.

For the first time since he was a cub, he had all the pleasure of exploring the ground with his feet, of sharpening his claws on trees, of covering his scat by drawing earth and stones over it, of receiving all the exciting messages the surface of the world has to offer any normal cat. All the rest of his senses seemed clearer. With his four feet in touch with the ground, he could smell better, and his instincts and reflexes came back to him.

When something delicious-smelling ran unwarily past him, he found he had pounced on it and pinned it down without thought. He lay down with it between his front paws and played with it awhile before eating it. His claws clung to the meat. He kept sheathing and unsheathing them with a feeling of intense wellbeing, and used them to rip off its fur. Food brought to him ready killed had never, never tasted as this did. Fangs or no fangs, he crunched it up to the last bite and then lay licking his pads and between his toes. It was a feeling like no other. He did it for a long time, until every part of his feet became his own again.

After his meal he needed to drink, and he could smell water not far off. He wandered down a hill and found that his way to the water was barred by a wall. He sprang over it easily, his new claws helping at the top. He was in the garden of a villa. In the middle of the garden was a pool with a small fountain. He drank his fill, and then lay down on the paving to sleep. Of course, he felt no fear of the two-legs that he could smell everywhere.

A scream awoke him and he raised his head. A female two-legs was standing not far away from him in an archway, mouth wide, making peacock shrieks. Boots was up and over the wall in a flash of gold and black.

But the sight of the female two-legs reminded him of *his* female two-legs. He felt a need of her, for she was part of his life. He began to quest the air for her special smell.

Sightings of the runaway tiger were not limited to the woman at the villa with the fountain. Several people saw him, and reported back to Caesar's messengers who were ranging over and around the city offering rewards to anyone who could catch the beast or give information leading to his capture. But Boots was showing unexpected cunning. He had several hiding places where he lay up during the day, and he only came out at night to hunt and explore and search the air for telltale hints of Aurelia in the wind.

After a week, the search was given up. No one had seen the tiger for three days at this point and it was assumed he had left the district and run into the rough country to the south. Caesar was furious. He had invested large sums in the hunt, and the animal itself was very valuable. Besides, he was not used to being thwarted. The longer Boots seemed to defy his hunters, the deeper became Caesar's anger, and having no other target, it fixed itself on Julius. The four cage-slaves were swiftly disposed of, but Julius had to be kept alive until Caesar decided on a suitable fate for him. Meanwhile he contented himself with throwing him into a prison adjoining the Colosseum to await his fate.

★

Aurelia, although terribly afraid of the outcome, did what she had to do. Despite her mother's pleadings and warnings, she went to see her father.

"Father, I have something very important to tell you."

"What is it? I'm extremely busy just now."

"It's about my tiger."

He looked up from the table where he was working. There were some new lines, like slashes, across his forehead and between his eyes.

"Well?"

"It wasn't the fault of – of the slave Julius. It was my fault."

"Indeed. How?"

"I – I took Boots away and hid him, to play a joke on Julius."

"What was 'Julius' doing, meanwhile?"

"He'd slipped away for a moment."

"To relieve himself?"

"Yes, Father."

"Leaving you alone, but for four cage-slaves who were fast asleep."

Aurelia was silent.

"And your cousin, what part did he have in this – joke?"

"None! He was asleep too. It was my idea."

"A likely story," said Caesar. He bent again to his work, and waved a dismissive hand at her.

"But Father – it's true—"

He raised his head again, and gave her a look that froze her heart.

"It's a lie. A stupid, childish, unbelievable lie. You're just trying to protect your cousin – very touching, but pointless. The slave was to blame, whatever you two children did or didn't do. Leave me now and don't refer to this again if you don't want to make me seriously angry."

So the encounter that had taken all Aurelia's courage came to nothing.

It was no more difficult for Aurelia to find out where Julius was imprisoned than it had been for Marcus to get *his* information. The problem was contacting him without the knowledge of anyone who might betray her to her father.

In the end, it was her old nurse that she turned to.

Aurelia was in the habit of visiting her in her small apartment at the back of the palace, so the nurse suspected nothing when her "dear little precious" came knocking.

Her visitor had brought her sweetmeats and some fresh grapes, and also a small jug of wine, which the nurse liked perhaps more than she should.

"Why thank you, my little treasure!" She promptly poured herself a goblet of wine and quaffed it down, smacking her lips. "And how are you feeling today? Putting your troubles behind you, I hope?"

"No, Nurse. I'm still very unhappy."

"Ah, when you were a little toddling thing, how easy it was to rub and kiss your hurts away! Come and get a kiss from your old nurse anyhow, and tell me all about it."

Aurelia hugged her and sat close to her with her arm around her shoulders.

"Well, my sweet nurse, I've lost my pet tiger, but I don't complain of that. You know the boy who used to bring my tiger to see me?" The nurse sniffed disapprovingly, but nodded. "Father's very angry with him and has locked him up in chains. Of course, I know he has good reasons and always acts justly, but... I happen to know that... that boy, Julius his name is, is the only support of his mother, and – I thought – it must be so hard on her, poor woman, to think of her only son in prison. I wonder if... I know you know the prison governor."

"Oh, him! I know him all right. He'll do anything for me. He had his eye on me, years ago, when I was young and pretty. Plenty of men did, young themselves then and handsome, though they may not be so young now. And don't you dare smile!"

"I'm not smiling! I believe you, because you're still beautiful," said Aurelia earnestly. "So, what I'm asking is, could you find his mother and take her to the prison to visit him? See, I've written a note for her to offer my sympathy and say I might be able to help her... later." She pressed a small roll of papyrus into the nurse's hand, knowing she couldn't read. Probably Julius's mother couldn't, either, but with luck she would show it to Julius, for whom the message had been written. Julius could read a little, because during the long summer days when Boots lay asleep and there was nothing to do, Aurelia, for her own amusement, had taught him. It was not signed, and the handwriting was heavily disguised. It said simply, *Don't despair. You have a friend.*

The nurse took another drink of wine and examined the scroll, turning it about while Aurelia sat in suspense. Then she said cannily, "And I suppose I am not to mention this errand? Or let this little piece of writing, which doesn't look long enough to say what you told me it says, fall into the wrong hands?"

Aurelia hesitated, then nodded.

"And why is it a secret, may one ask? If it's just an innocent act of kindness on the part of Caesar's little daughter?"

Aurelia hadn't expected to be asked questions. She blushed and stuttered. "Well, because – because I don't think Mata and – and Father would approve of me interesting myself in – in a slave's... family."

"In his *family*? Or in him, my young madam? Which is it?"

Aurelia couldn't meet her suddenly sharp and penetrating eyes. She flung herself against the familiar soft bosom. "Oh Nurse! Oh Nurse!" was all she could mumble. But the old woman felt her trembling with suppressed sobs.

"Ah, there, there," she said gently, petting her. "I know. We can't always love only where we should. He's a handsome stripling. And I've seen how he looks at you." She heaved a monstrous sigh. "Dangerous work you set me to. Could you not forget him? For he's as good as dead, my dove. You know that and I know it. No, no. Don't cry. I'll do your errand. But leaving out the mother, I think. It will be quicker if I just visit *him*." She sat Aurelia upright and wiped her cheeks with the corner of her scarf. Then she picked up the scroll. "This is for him, I take it?" Aurelia nodded. The nurse tucked it into her dress, and sighed again. "The gods created wild beasts to be made into rugs and wall hangings, not pets. I said so, but who listens to an old woman?"

Aurelia threw her arms around the nurse's neck and hugged her until she pushed her off.

"I could get my death for this," she scolded. "You don't have to squeeze the life out of me first."

One day, Boots was seen in one of the side streets south of the city.

In hours, the whole of Rome fell into ferment. Citizens were afraid to leave their homes, or even to venture into their courtyards. There was a kind of hysteria in the air. Boots was confused in people's minds with Brute, the most ferocious man-eater ever seen in the circus.

The hunt was resumed, various traps were set, but without avail. As the days passed, the fear grew, and even streets in the heart of Rome became almost deserted at night. From merely stealing drinks from private fountains after dark, Boots became bolder. He began to stalk the empty streets, looking for small prey such as cats and dogs that strayed out of doors. He had lost weight but he was still a pampered house tiger, glad to get a meal without too much effort.

People missed their pets, of course, and rumours swiftly spread that the tiger was abroad in the heart of the city. Some even caught glimpses of his sinuous form, silhouetted against the light-coloured stone of which Rome was built, a sinister shadow sliding past walls and closed gates. Rumours of sightings spread like wildfire – rumour placed him in many different parts of the city, all at the same time, and so it began to be said that he had magic powers. People became all the more afraid of him.

And Caesar grew all the angrier. Soon the whole household was scurrying about like mice, trying to avoid him. Even Aurelia felt afraid of him.

Marcus came to see Aurelia at last. The agony of shame he felt had become too much to bear alone.

"What's happening to Julius?" was his first question as soon as they were able to creep away to their favourite courtyard and be alone.

"He's still in prison. Look."

She furtively passed him the small papyrus roll that the nurse had brought back from her clandestine visit to Julius's cell.

Marcus snatched it and read it. "How did you get this?" he asked breathlessly.

She told him. He looked down again. The writing under her writing – scrawling and ill-spelt like a child's – said: *The date is set. The ides of July. No friend however dear and true can help me. Look after my mother.* The ides of July! That meant the middle day of the month. "But that's in fourteen days!" Marcus cried.

"Shhh. Yes. We have to find a way to help him, Marcus."

"You mean because we'll never stop feeling guilty."

Something seemed to break in her.

"That doesn't matter! What matters is, Julius will be dead, and by some horrible way! I can't bear it, Marcus, I can't bear it!"

He stared at her. He saw she was distraught, and suddenly understood something of what she had been going through while he sat at home with his little portion of shame.

"I don't see how we can do anything," he muttered uneasily. "They think we're only children. No one will listen to us."

"I'm not a child any more," she said. And he looked at her and was awed to see that it was true. "Marcus, maybe if you talked to your father, he could influence mine. You must confess. They'd believe both of us."

"Are you mad? My father already suspects I had something to do with it! If he found out what we did,

I'd be dreadfully punished! He'd beat me, for sure!"

"Would a beating be as bad as Julius dying? I'd gladly be beaten if it would save him!" She was pacing the floor, wringing her hands, her tears almost spouting from her eyes. Marcus thought of his sweat falling on the face of the goddess.

"Have there been any omens?" he asked. "Have you consulted the entrails?"

She stopped pacing. She stood still for a full minute. Then she looked him in the face.

"I'm going to tell you something. Something you mustn't tell anyone."

"I could keep any secret now!" he said grimly.

"I think I might be becoming a Christian."

His jaw dropped, not merely from astonishment but from horror.

She went on, "The Christians don't think the circus is right. They're against it."

"Well, they would be! They're put to death there!"

"I know. It's terrible. They're helpless. Women and little children, being smeared with blood to make sure the beasts attack them!"

"Their men are cowards, though! When they're given weapons, they refuse to fight."

"They're martyrs."

"What's a martyr?"

"Someone who allows themselves to be killed because of their beliefs."

He looked at her, baffled and aghast. Such a concept was completely beyond him.

"Why would anyone do that?"

"Wouldn't you let yourself be killed for the sake of Rome?"

"Not if I could get out of it!" he answered promptly.

"Well, the Christians don't try to get out of it. They submit themselves, to prove that they're strong in their beliefs. They believe they're going to somewhere called Heaven after they die. It's a bit like Olympus. They believe they're going to live with their god."

Marcus shook his head as if to clear it of a fog of incomprehension. "That's complete rubbish. Anyway, how do you know all this?"

"From my tutors. I've been asking them questions. Of course, they tell it to me to teach me how powerful Rome is, and how stupid and weak and mistaken the Christians are. And because," she added with sudden fierceness, "those old men enjoy talking about all those awful things. They're disgusting. They gloat over the suffering of those poor people. If my tutors only knew what I'm really learning!"

"What do you mean?" asked Marcus, more and more alarmed.

"That it's possible to be against the circus, not because you're afraid to die there, but because it's wicked and wrong."

Marcus walked unsteadily away from her. He pretended it was just so that he could go to a couch and sit down, but the impulse was to get as far from her and the contamination of her mad ideas as he decently could. What she was saying filled him with fear. The Christians were outcasts – enemies to the state. If Aurelia was serious in what she said, he had a clear duty to—

To what? Betray her? Impossible. Oh, why was she doing this to him, putting him into this horrible position?

"You shouldn't have told me," he muttered.

"I had to tell someone. I tried to tell my nurse, but she wouldn't listen."

"She was right. Do you want to be a traitor to Rome? To your *own father*?"

"My father," she said, "is going to put Julius to death for what *we* did."

"He doesn't know it was us."

"Yes, he does. I've confessed already."

"You haven't!" he breathed in horror.

"Yes, but don't worry about yourself – he didn't care. He's determined to kill Julius." Her voice dropped. "I started to stop loving him that day at the circus. He's cruel, and the things he does, and allows, are terrible and wrong. I can't love him now, even if he is my father."

CHAPTER THIRTEEN

Aurelia's Sacrifice

As each day passed until the ides of July, Aurelia became more and more desperate.

She had no idea how to pray to the Christian god, so she was forced back upon her old ones. As far back as memory went, she had been accustomed, each day as a matter of routine, to placing offerings of food and drink at the *larium* – the wooden shrine with its complement of small figures of the household deities. Of course, the food stayed where she put it until it was cleared away by the servants, but Aurelia understood that the gods didn't need real food, only its spiritual essence. It was the offering that mattered, not the substance.

But now matters were so desperate that the ordinary gifts didn't seem enough. What was food to her, after all? She had all the food she needed. A real sacrifice was required.

She took out her jewellery and chose her favourite – a bracelet that her mother had given her years ago. She had always loved it. It was a gorgeous thing delicately fashioned of gold and hung with bells that tinkled as she moved her arm. The clapper of each bell was a tiny ruby.

She stood before the *larium* and contemplated. If she laid the bracelet there, her mother would see it, or the servants would report it. In any case – did the Roman gods, the gods of her family, want such baubles? Did lifeless gold have a spiritual essence?

Perhaps the Christian god would appreciate it? The Christians had only one god, but he was said to be all-powerful, commanding all lesser gods. Yes. A king of gods required golden tokens, surely, as all rulers did. But how to give it to him? Give it finally and unrecoverably?

She thought deeply – as deeply as prayer. And inspiration came. She would throw it into the Tiberis.

The Tiberis was Rome's river, on which the city depended for water – for life itself – and as such, of course, was itself sacred. That would be perfect. Her sacrifice would be both to the old gods, and her secret new one – surely *some* powerful being would be won over by her deed! She wrapped the bracelet in a silken cloth and crept from the palace.

The river ran not too far away. Her feet in their house-sandals tapped on the rounded cobbles. Once she slipped, and the precious offering flew from her hand, but she recovered it, and nobody saw her because there were no citizens abroad. It was twilight. It was the first time in her life that Aurelia had ever come out of the palace unaccompanied. As the shadows lengthened, she became aware of her recklessness. She had never seen the streets so empty. She didn't know it was the Time of the Tiger. She had almost forgotten Boots in her passionate anxiety about his keeper.

Soon she stood on a great stone bridge that spanned the river, which was in spate. The snow melt that came down from the mountains of the north had filled its tributaries and now it was at its highest and swiftest. She gazed down into the sacred waters.

"Oh gods, all of you, great ones – hear and help me!" she said under her breath. "Save Julius. Let him be spared. I ask nothing more and will never ask anything more. Take my offering." She held the silk by one corner, and watched the flash of gold as the beloved bracelet turned over and over and entered the tumbling waters without even a splash.

Prayer is easy, she thought. *Deeds are harder.* A tear fell – a minute addition to the rushing river. Then she looked upwards.

"God of the brave Christians," she whispered. "It was for you. I don't dare to anger our Roman gods, but it was really for you. I can't sacrifice my life – I dare not even turn to you openly. I'm too big a coward. I don't see why you should accept my prayer," she added humbly. "Julius isn't a Christian, and you don't save the poor people who accept a horrible death for your sake. But—"

She stopped suddenly. She'd seen a movement on the far bank. There! Among the reeds. There – again! A striped coat – a long tail – a great head, stooping to drink. Could it be? The answer to her prayer, so quickly?

"Boots!" It was a scream, to carry above the noise of the river. "Boots!"

She rushed headlong off the bridge and on to the riverside path, then down the sloping stones to the edge of the water where the reeds grew – where her tiger was standing, knee-deep in the river, lifting his dripping face to look at her.

"Boots! It's me! Come, come, my sweet old darling, come." She made swishing sounds to call him, and put her hand out.

For a moment it seemed he would not come. Then he caught her scent. With one bound he was at her side, rubbing his wet face against her thigh, feeling the familiar caresses on his ears, on his shoulders, along his back.

"Oh, Boots, you've lost your collar! And your boots are gone! Oh, you bad boy, where have you been?" She knelt beside him and hugged him around his neck. She felt the rough grating of his tongue on her cheek. He could have taken her head off with one good bite. Instead he purred, pushed his head under her chin, and knocked her over.

She scrambled to her feet. Her face was shining with incredulous happiness.

"Come, Boots! Come along! We're going home. We're going to save Julius!"

She led him back through the empty streets. If anyone was watching through their casements they would have seen their princess striding by, her long hair and diaphanous garments lifted by the breeze, the great striped beast at her side, her hand on its neck – they looked like figures on a painted vase or in a sacred mosaic: she a goddess, the tiger her devotee.

She entered the palace through the front entrance. The guards stood aside, astonished and awed. She rushed straight to her parents' apartments.

"Father! Mata! Come and see!"

Her mother and father emerged from their rooms. They stopped dead at the sight of the girl and the tiger standing together in the glittering, lamp-lit antechamber.

Caesar recovered first.

"So – you've found him. Thank the gods for that, now the city can remember itself and get back to normal. Where was he?"

"Down by the river!" She was too happy and excited to be guarded. Only when she saw her parents exchange shocked glances did she remember that she was strictly forbidden to go out alone. "Pata, Mata, I had to! I had something very, very important to do! I had to make a sacrifice to – to the gods, a real sacrifice, and say my prayers to the Tiberis! And look! The gods heard me and answered!" The tiger had sat himself down beside her and was licking one of his forepaws calmly, making a spitting noise as he cleaned between his toes. Aurelia's arm was about his neck and she was smiling, as it seemed, with her whole body.

For a moment Caesar, faced with this happy pair, weakened in his resolve. His wife was looking at him beseechingly. *Relent! Relent! Look how happy she is! Don't spoil it!* But his word had gone from him.

"You can't keep him, my girl," he said stiffly, hardening his heart. "You must see for yourself, it's too dangerous." He watched her face fall, her arm drop. He saw her begin to tremble. But he went on: "I take my share of the blame, for having thought a wild beast a suitable present. You've had many months of pleasure with him, but now he must make up to Rome for having filled its citizens with fear by his escape."

"Make up to Rome? How?"

"By going into the arena, of course."

For a moment there was silence. Then Aurelia screamed. "What! *What?* You'll put him in your hateful circus to be *killed*?"

Caesar felt anger rise in him hotly. Was she defying him? His own daughter? Neither of his sons would have dared!

"I will," he said fiercely. "And his keeper with him."

The girl stood perfectly still, all colour draining from her face. "But you can't," she whispered. "Not now I've brought Boots back. Not after I told you that it was me

who let him escape. You can't hurt Julius now. It would
be too cruel. Too unjust."

There was a frozen silence. Caesar could not believe
his own ears. Nor could he credit what his brain was
telling him. If the tiger had not been there, beside her,
he would have rushed upon his child and struck her.

"Why should you care what happens to a slave?"

Aurelia opened her lips.

Her mother, galvanised by the potential horror of
the situation, tried to intervene, but Caesar halted her
with one imperious gesture.

"Speak the truth!" he barked suddenly.

But Aurelia dared not say the words. She fell to her
knees just as Julius had, her head down, her hands over
her face. A long, long moment, a moment of paralysis,
passed.

"You will see my justice," said Caesar, in a voice
terrifyingly empty of all emotion. "Yes. You will *see* it. You
won't be spared. If I have to hold your eyes open with my
own hands, you will witness every second of it."

CHAPTER FOURTEEN

The Ides of July

The day had come.

Marcus woke early and went out on to his balcony that overlooked the countryside through which Boots had made his escape. Of course he knew that the tiger had been found by Aurelia (her lone pilgrimage was the subject of scandal and gossip throughout the city), that Caesar had sent him to the Colosseum. He knew that today was the day that the animal he had so often petted, and felt jealous of, and admired, was surely going to die. Under other circumstances he would have been sorry for it.

But Marcus knew that Julius would die today, too. There was no doubt or hope in his mind about it.

Caesar had ordered that he be sent unarmed into the arena to be torn to pieces by the other tiger, the terrible man-eater. And Marcus also knew that his cousin would be there when it happened, with the eyes of Rome upon her to see how she bore herself.

Of course none of the vast crowd who would be there today would know that she wasn't there of her own free will, but had been condemned to watch the spectacle as a punishment. But Marcus knew. When he let himself imagine her feelings this morning, his brain twisted away, as his body might from a lighted brand thrust into his face.

He hadn't done as she asked, and spoken to his father the senator. And this was a dreadful burden on him. She had confessed, she had begged him to do the same, but he hadn't dared. Besides, his father had not been available. Dangerous events were afoot in the Empire – events that, ordinarily, Marcus would have been very excited about: the legions on the march against barbarian invaders from the East, and the Senate in session much of the time. The only concern anyone in authority had with the circus at this time of crisis was that it should keep the populous from too much concern about the military situation, which had called many of their men away.

As Marcus stood there looking out across the hills, his father suddenly came into the room behind him.

"Marcus!"

He turned around, startled and nervous.

"Yes, Father?"

"I suppose you'll want to go to the circus this afternoon?"

He stood open-mouthed.

"The whole city is talking about it! The two tigers will fight to the death. Surely you want to see that?"

"One of them is Aurelia's tiger," mumbled Marcus, looking at his sandalled feet.

"Well of course I know that," said the senator impatiently. "That should make it more interesting for you! Do you want to go or don't you?"

Marcus was aware that his father was looking at him very searchingly. If he refused, for any reason, it would only confirm his suspicions that Marcus had something to hide.

"All right, Father. I-I'd like to go."

"Very well, you can go with Caesar's party. The Emperor has invited you."

And why did he do that? Marcus wondered. *Is he trying to punish me as well as Relia?* He dreaded the thought of being there – dreaded it.

But something in him – the manhood he was growing towards – was glad. Last time, he had been waiting for his cousin to show fear, *wanting her to* so that he could feel superior. Last time, Julius had been with her, Julius had supported and comforted her. This time – this time, when she would need far more comfort – perhaps she would turn to Marcus.

And anyway, it was only right that he should share her ordeal. It was his just deserts.

Aurelia had not emerged from her apartment since the encounter with her father.

Her personal servants tiptoed in and out with meals she refused to touch. She didn't undress or wash herself. She paced the floor, crying and tearing her clothes. She slept very little, and then often lying on the cold marble floor, not on her bed. She was trying, perhaps, to imitate the conditions of Julius in his prison cell. She strove to fill her thoughts with a more powerful emotion than fear or the horrible apprehension of what was to come. They were filled with bitter, furious hatred for her father, who had unlimited power to do good or harm, and chose harm.

When her mother came to see her and remonstrate with her – "Look at yourself! Have you no self-respect?" – she turned on her.

"You're his wife. You can influence him."

"No! I can't."

"Women have ways. I've heard. You can refuse him—"

Her mother shrank away from her. "How can you speak of such things? Your father's right! I think you've lost your mind, not just your silly heart! Where's your duty and obedience? Has my example taught you nothing?"

"I refuse to be dutiful to a man I hate!"

"*Aurelia!* It's blasphemy to hate the Emperor, even if he were not your father!"

"Can it be blasphemy to hate what's wicked and cruel? It's not only Julius. It's everything. It's the circus. It's the animals. It's the *Christians!*" She was on the very verge of telling her mother her secret, but, luckily for her, her mother was already rushing from the room, her hands over her ears.

Now the dreaded day had come.

Caesar sent a male messenger early in the morning.

"Princess, Caesar orders you to ready yourself."

"Tell him I won't."

The man looked away in distress. He could scarcely believe the sight before him – Rome's beautiful princess, her hair dirty, tangled and uncombed, her clothes draggled and torn, her face thin and wild.

"Caesar's orders are," he muttered, "if you will not ready yourself, servants will be sent to wash and dress you by force."

She knew then that it was hopeless. Her pleas had failed. The condition she'd fallen into as proof of her despair, had failed. He would make her go through with it. If he had to tie her up and have her carried to the Colosseum — if, as he'd threatened, he had to stand behind her and force her eyes open — he would make it happen, he would make her watch it. There was no escape but one, to take her own life — and she knew she couldn't do that.

In her desperation she did a fierce and terrible thing. She ran to the *larium,* the shrine that had been her reverence since childhood, and, throwing open the wooden doors, tore out the sacred figures with both hands and hurled them to the ground with a sickening crash.

"Tell him! Tell my father what I've done!" she screamed at the messenger. "Tell him I worship the Christian god now, and that god hates him as much as I do!"

The messenger gasped in horror, and fled. He told no one the incredible thing he had seen, the impossible things she had said. He was afraid to utter the words for fear the gods would punish him.

Aurelia waited, her whole body clenched and trembling, for the people who would come and force her to do her father's will.

Instead, the nurse came.

She entered in a rush, swept to the middle of the floor where the girl sat, hunched and stiff, ready to resist to the last. She gasped at the sight of her, but she said nothing, merely bent down, lifted her to her feet with surprising strength, and smacked her hard through her torn clothes.

"Come. *Come at once*," she ordered.

Aurelia found herself half led, half dragged into her private bathroom. The nurse removed her dress and threw it into a corner. She pushed Aurelia down the two steps, forced her to sit in the square stone basin, then clapped her hands. Servants, obviously primed beforehand, entered with warm water in copper ewers. The nurse dismissed them, rolled up her sleeves, and proceeded to wash Aurelia as if she were four years old. She rubbed her with oil, scraped her with a strigil, scrubbed her hands and feet with pumice and washed her hair, pouring jug after jug of water over her. Aurelia sat under the ministrations, familiar from her early childhood, and felt the fight drain out of her body as the water washed over it. The nurse pulled her to her feet at the end and wrapped her in a huge, absorbent sheet. With another she briskly rubbed her hair till it hung in a dark, damp cloud, then pulled a comb through it and, with the aid of long ivory pins, arranged it on her head like a grown woman.

"Now," she said, "what is being worn this season, for the worst that can possibly happen?"

Aurelia gave a cry of pain and flung herself against the nurse. But she pushed her upright, gripping her arms.

"Stop that," she said sternly. She pinioned her with her eyes. "This is the testing time. Now you will prove that you are the daughter of an Emperor, no matter what you think of him. Now you will show whose milk built you – that you are *my nursling.*"

She led her back into the bed chamber. She stopped short, and lost colour, when she noticed for the first time the broken gods on the ground, but she said nothing. She dressed Aurelia in her most beautiful dress, the finest imported silk in bright, eye-catching colours banded with gold thread, and draped a contrasting *palla* around her shoulders.

"When your Julius enters the arena," she said as she

did so, "he will look up at the Royal Box. He will see you there. Is the last thing he looks at going to be a cowering, weeping, defeated little wretch, made ugly by hate and sorrow? No. He will see his princess, beautiful, strong and proud, and – yes, I will say it, may the gods forgive me – with her eyes full of love for him. It will be a sight to give him courage to face what he must. That's what you can do for him now. No. Be still and listen to me. Nothing can change what the gods have decreed. Accept their will. What did I tell you when you were a little girl? The only way we women can get through our lives honourably is with courage and resignation, both."

She put the finishing touches to Aurelia's appearance, fastening a diadem across her forehead, a jewelled pendant round her neck, and gold bangles on her wrists. Aurelia stood motionless, numb now, unable to feel anything but the deep dread of what the next few hours would bring.

"Your cousin's waiting," said the nurse.

Aurelia started from her apathy.

"Marcus? Marcus is here? He's – coming?"

The nurse nodded. A tiny fraction of Aurelia's burden of anguish lifted. At least she would not be quite alone, with no one who knew what she felt.

"And you? Will you be there?" she asked piteously.

"Me? I have never set foot in that nasty place and I never will, not till I turn Christian and they feed *me* to the lions," the nurse replied.

Aurelia stared at her for a moment and then walked, unsteadily but with a straight back, out of the room.

The nurse heaved one of her profound sighs, and set about clearing up the debris of the broken gods. She thought there were one or two she might be able to repair. There was one small *lar* – a jolly godling whose responsibility was the welfare of the family – which, being made of bronze, had escaped the destruction. She looked at him. He held a cornucopia in one hand, a drinking vessel in the other, had vine leaves in his hair and a swinging tunic to show he was dancing. Breathing a prayer, she put him back in his place, and closed the doors of the *larium* gently. Then she left the palace by the servants' way.

Nobody ever questioned her comings and goings.

CHAPTER FIFTEEN

In the Arena

The Colosseum was packed to its rounded walls. Forty-five thousand spectators filled the tiers of seats. Another five thousand found standing room. The vast canvas awning kept the worst of the sun off the highest-paying citizens; the rest sat or stood in its full blaze.

The arena itself bore a likeness to an African desert – sand reflecting whitely back at the pitiless sky, not a mark yet on the smooth surface, as if no living creature had ever trodden there, as if it waited for the marks that the living would make – innocent of its prime function, to soak up the blood of the dying.

As usual the expectant crowd, chaotically loud a

moment before, fell silent as Caesar's party appeared through the back of the Royal Box, and then burst into concerted roars of adulation.

Aurelia didn't wait for her father to indicate where she was to sit – she took her own place, as far from him as possible, indicating to Marcus the seat beside her. She realised now that her father wouldn't really stand behind her and hold her eyes open, as he had threatened. It would demean him to do so. But suddenly she became aware that a member of the Praetorian Guard was standing behind her. Had he had orders...? No. No man would dare lay a hand on her. Or would he? The thought absolutely terrified her and she clutched Marcus's hand convulsively.

Below, in the cells, corridors and cages under the innocently raked sand, all was purposeful bustle and organised activity.

Scores of half-clad, huge-muscled men hurried to and fro in the torch-lit darkness, unconscious of the overpowering stench of distressed animals, and their own sweat. The beasts patrolled their cages, well aware that they were on some perilous edge.

Boots alone had no premonition of battle, hurt and death. The smells around him carried no lethal meaning. He sniffed them curiously. They were like those he was accustomed to in the menagerie, but with something added, an element he couldn't identify. He couldn't know it was the smell of fear.

A cage was manhandled past his cage. And suddenly he stiffened and rose to his feet.

In the cage was another like himself.

A strong new smell assailed him. A smell that stirred something in his brain. Something familiar there? Something remembered from long ago?

The cage trundled past and was gone.

Boots lay down, but feeling excited he stood up again and began to prowl, round and round in his narrow prison. Something in that scent had set his nerves alight. The familiar smell lingered faintly. Into his brain came dim remembered sensations. A warmth along his side. A face rubbing against his, whiskers blending, sending messages of comfort. Communications such as he'd never had with any other creature.

He kept turning his face to where he had last seen his fellow beast in the cage.

Brute hadn't noticed anything. He was on his way to fight, and to feast. That was all he knew and all he wanted to know. He felt little fear, for he knew what was afoot and that for him, it would be satisfying. He would snarl, pounce, kill and eat. The roaring from all around him would urge him on.

He willingly walked from his "travelling" cage to the three-sided one on the platform that would carry him aloft. The open side was swiftly turned to face the brick wall. Then he was left alone. Soon, other two-legs would come to do the mysterious things that would hoist him to the surface of the arena. Everything was as it always was before he went *up there*.

Then something happened that was not usual.

The two-legs who had taught him to be angry was suddenly standing beside the cage. He spoke his name.

"Here, Brute. Look what I've got for you."

Brute's attention was caught. There was no tigerish growl now in his tormentor's voice. He had his pointed stick, but it didn't jab at him. On the end of it was a piece of fresh meat.

The tiger watched it poke through the bars of the cage and as soon as he could reach it, he snatched it with his claws and gulped it down.

"Good boy," said the two-legs. Then he went away. Brute lay down to lick his chops. Soon the other two-legs came and got ready to winch the cage up to the surface.

★

In the dark, noisome corridor, the nurse waited for Caius.

"Did you do it?"

"Yes, may the gods help me."

"Was it a nice big piece?"

"Do you want him to lie down and go to sleep up there? No. It was a small piece. Even that could have me thrown in the cage with him."

"Don't worry, my dear friend! No one will ever know. You're a good fellow." She reached up and kissed him, as she had often done long ago, when they were young. Not that they felt old now. He reached for her, but she evaded his arms.

"You won't forget the other business?"

"No! Not that. I can't, Bella – I daren't!"

She reached into the folds of cloth at her breast and brought out a bag chinking with coins. It was her life's savings, but Caius was not to know that. His eyes fastened greedily upon the bag and his hand reached out without his order.

"Just do it for me, my dear old love," whispered the nurse.

The coins in his hand, he stared at her, helpless before his own cupidity. She tapped his grizzled cheek playfully, and slipped away, back to the palace.

She was not happy – not at all. Or hopeful of a happy outcome. But she'd done what she could, and that had to be her comfort until it was all over.

Julius was saying his prayers. His body was taut and trembling with fear. But his brain was clear.

He stood in his waiting-cell with head bowed and asked the gods to give him courage. Not strength – strength would be useless. He didn't intend to give extra pleasure to the crowd by resisting. All he wanted was to die bravely.

Then he thanked the gods for his life, and for the love he felt for the princess. Though it was a forbidden love, still he felt it to be the worthiest thing about him, and the purest, and the deepest. He asked the gods to take care of his mother, and of Aurelia.

At last, he reviewed his life. Truly, he had nothing to be ashamed of – until that fateful moment when he had fallen asleep in the sun. What little weaknesses can bring about a man's downfall! He didn't resent his doom. He knew that to have risked the princess's life was deserving of death.

But this death?

Why not? Many just as good as he and better had

walked this road. He had watched it happen. The lion sprang, the man fell under its weight, the beast generally mauled him, especially if he struggled – a cat's instinct to play with its prey – and then it would bite and claw him until shock and pain and loss of blood killed him. Julius wouldn't struggle. He would copy the Christians, he would stand straight for as long as he could and then—

He heard the crowd roar.

The beast that would be his executioner must have been released. He quaked with dread, but in the midst of it he remembered something. He remembered that he had once had the peculiar thought that if he were to be eaten by a beast, he would spare a prayer for it, too.

"May the gods look kindly on the beast that is to kill me. May it live out its life even if I can't."

He smiled at himself. What a strange prayer! Yet while he was making it, for those brief seconds, he forgot his terror.

But it returned.

His time had come. He dragged a deep, rough breath, that rattled over his fear like the sea over pebbles, and stiffened himself.

Two guards threw open the door of his cell. They gave him no chance to walk with dignity, but dragged him along the corridors and swiftly up some steps to a barred gate leading directly into the arena. Through it, Julius could see his appointed killer, standing on the far side, under the Royal Box; his bright stripes were like nature's danger signal.

A strange wash of pride covered Julius's fear for a moment. Not an ignominious death then, in the foul breath of hyenas or even at the teeth of the common lion. Nothing less than the great man-eating tiger! Something for the crowds, indeed! At least his death might be remembered – for an hour or two.

And then something totally unlooked-for happened. One of the guards put a sword into his hand.

Julius looked down at it stupidly. He was to be given the chance to defend himself! But he was no gladiator. What was the use of a sword to him? Yet he clutched it, as a man must clutch the slightest hope.

The rattle of chains... The gate opened upwards and he was pushed forward. A moment later it clanged shut behind him.

The crowd fell silent. Sunlight poured down, as if the gods were flooding the arena with a light fiercer than usual, the better to watch the show from their Olympian heights. The tiger standing thirty paces from Julius turned its head, and gazed at him. It began to move slowly towards him. When it had covered half the distance between them, Julius's mouth fell open.

That wasn't Brute! It was Boots.

Boots! His tiger! But changed – no longer plump and sleek, but thin and hungry-looking. His head hung low, his tail twitched. From his throat came deep sounds. Not growls. A singing whine. Julius knew that sound, he had once or twice interpreted it for Aurelia: "*Now listen to him! He's saying, 'I'm not happy, I'm bewildered, reassure me!'*"

Julius dropped the sword in the sand.

The crowd gasped.

He walked towards the tiger with one hand – his sword hand – held out. The raked sand had never received the imprint of such strides towards danger.

Boots smelt him coming. He ran the last steps and rose on his hind feet, his head and up-stretched paws high above Julius's head. The crowd cried out in an ecstasy of anticipation. But when the great paws came down, they fell *gently* on to the man's unprotected shoulders, and he didn't fall backwards, he stood his ground, and... and...

Now the crowd rose to its feet in waves of audible disbelief.

The man was caressing the tiger's ears, he was

smiling, he was talking to it! The beast was rubbing its face against the man's jaw!

Aurelia and Marcus were unashamedly clinging to each other, their eyes, huge with suspense, fixed on the scene being played out directly below them.

As the vast crowd broke into shouts and roars – of astonishment, delight, and approval – Aurelia jumped up. Her eyes still riveted to the beloved pair in the ring, she forced her way among the other guests in the Royal Box to her father's side and tried to hug him.

"Oh, Pata! That's Boots! You knew he wouldn't hurt him. Thank you! Thank you! I love you after all – I love—"

Her father, without even looking at her, pushed her away so violently that she almost fell.

"Watch!"

It was a command.

She backed away. The other guests, shocked, made way for her and in a moment she was back in her seat beside Marcus.

He wasn't looking at her. His eyes were on the ring.

"Oh, Relia," he muttered hollowly. "Look."

She looked. For a moment she doubted her senses. There were two tigers in that vast space. Another had appeared as if from nowhere – from the ground.

Boots turned his head first, because he had caught that scent again. That familiar, tantalising evocation of intimacy in another place and time. He turned to face the newcomer who was bounding straight towards them, low to the ground, with unmistakable intent.

Boots moved forward, in front of Julius, who stood stock-still, petrified.

Brute stopped almost in mid-spring. The two stood a tiger's length apart, gazing at each other. Boots uttered a low whine.

Brute roared, the fur on his shoulders erect, his lips clear of his fangs.

He feinted to one side, as if to spring, but the other stood in his path.

Boots advanced towards his brother. Brute put his head on one side and roared. He was baffled. The other tiger kept creeping closer, belly touching the ground, eyes down, making a low, sing-song sound. Now he could smell him. He was of his blood – yes. But there was something strange. Male, and yet not male. And there was no threat. No sign of challenge.

When Boots got very close, he lay down and rolled over on his back in the posture of submission.

Brute backed off, bewildered. Beyond, the two-legs was within easy reach. He had no pointed stick. He was defenceless. Brute could smell him through the disturbing brother-smell. Every instinct and all his experience told him this was his prey. But between them lay this *other*.

From all around, a developing mutter arose. Fifty thousand people in the stands were growing impatient. The amusing novelty of a tame tiger and a magician was over. The man-eater was here! They wanted what they'd paid for — a battle, a death.

Brute knew that sound. It acted on him like the jabs from the pointed stick, provoking him. Hesitation and bafflement were overcome. With a snarl, he leapt over the supine body before him and launched himself at the two-legs.

In that fateful moment, as the terrifying shape seemed to fly through the air towards him, all Julius's determination to die without resisting was overwhelmed by his instinct to save himself.

His body took charge. It leapt aside. The black and gold shape flew past, landed, and turned. But Julius had turned too, and run — towards the glint in the sand. The sword! The tiger was behind him, close, but not running as fast as he might have done without a lump of meat in his stomach. Julius braked – the sword lay at his feet – he swooped on it, snatched it up, clutching the pommel through a handful of sand that fell back in a shower.

The crowd shouted its approval.

Julius just had time to turn – he was only half on his feet – before Brute leapt on him. In total terror Julius turned his head aside and screwed up his eyes, but his hands functioned without his orders, bracing the sword against his chest.

Brute leapt on to it. *When you leap against the sharp point, it is not there.*

But this time, it was.

The weight twisted the sword to one side, and knocked Julius to the ground. But it had wounded the tiger in the chest, deeply enough to make him back away with a furious yowl. The first blood of the day spotted the sand.

Julius regained his feet with a mighty effort. The tiger stood off, his snarling head writhing like a snake and all his claws extended, swiping at the sword. Julius jumped back, away from those scimitar claws, sweat standing out all over his body, every nerve electric with the urge to flee. *Run! Run!*

Suddenly through the tumult, from above his head,

he heard Aurelia screaming: "Fight, Julius! Fight!"

Julius dared not take his eyes for one split second from the tiger. But now he knew she was there. Her words sank into him like a barb and dragged him towards valour. He took a better grip on his sword. Yes! He must fight. He would lose, of course. But he *must fight*. He planted his shifting feet and straightened his body so that he stood up to his full height.

And then an incredulous realisation came to him.

He knew what his enemy was thinking.

Not for nothing had Julius spent hours with Boots, learning his language, translating it for the princess. Now, what was this tiger in front of him saying? He looked at the yellow glaring eyes, the writhing head, the lashing tail. The swiping forepaw. All said *I'm angry! I'm in pain! I want revenge!* But there was something more. There must be, or he would spring. What was it...?

I'm uncertain. I'm afraid.

Keeping his eyes fixed on Brute's eyes, Julius, calling on all his courage, forced his foot to take a step forward.

As he did it he noticed the tiniest movement in the animal. A shrinking – only a fraction, but it was a flinch. He knew that for this moment, and probably no longer, he was the dominant one. He took another step and pointed the sword directly at the tiger's face. This was a battle of wills, and with his special understanding, there was just a faint chance he could win.

Brute crouched, wriggling his hips, willing himself to pounce. But the two-legs' eyes were fixed on his. Brute could not meet those eyes.

He looked away.

Julius felt his heart leap with excitement. He understood the movement! In his head he explained to Aurelia: "*You see? He's saying, 'Why aren't you afraid of me? Men who aren't afraid of me are more powerful than I am.'*" He took another step forward. Around him, he sensed the crowd, absolutely silent, paralysed with suspense.

"Brute!"

Brute looked at him for a second, startled. His name!

"Go back. Go back. Go back."

At each order, another step forward.

The tiger felt the command in every nerve and sinew. This two-legs was his master. He began to back away, slowly, belly to the sand, giving that same sing-song whine. The whine his brother had given. The sound of submission.

"*What's he saying now, Julius?*"

"*Now he's saying, 'You've got the better of me. But beware. Look away, and I will take you!'*"

"Then don't! Don't look away! I want you to live!"

The dialogue was going on in his head, but in very truth she was up there, above him, in the Royal Box. She was watching. She had called to him, acknowledged him. His veins ran hot with courage and hope.

The tiger went back and back. When he was far enough away, he lay down in the sand and dropped his head on his paws. Then he rolled on his side and, tucking in his chin, began licking at his wound. There was no fight left in him – he had surrendered. Slowly, in a gesture of conquest, Julius lowered the point of his sword.

CHAPTER SIXTEEN

A Triumph of Will

The crowd seemed to explode. The whole Colosseum was filled with standing, cheering Romans.

Julius turned to face the Royal Box. Through the sweat running into his eyes he saw Aurelia, beautiful in her brave bright colours, standing now, her hands to her face, tears on her cheeks. She was weeping for him!

He saw the guests and guards, standing too, straining forward, some nearly falling over the rail as they cheered him.

He saw the Emperor. He alone was not cheering or showing the slightest emotion. He stood erect as if frozen amid the hysterical crowd in his box and around it – all around the vast arena.

Julius saluted and bowed. The crowd screamed with joy and waved their arms and threw objects into the air. Julius could see that the Emperor — that tiger among men — was baffled, as Brute had been. He had determined on Julius's death. He had only to give the signal and the ring would fill with merciless killers, who could put an end to him in an instant. He could see from the Emperor's face that it was in his mind, that he longed to use his power.

But he could not go against the people. Not when they were in this mood. Not when invaders were threatening the Empire and the populous had to be placated.

Slowly, with grinding reluctance, he did what he had to do. He took off his wreath of laurels and with a stiff, furious gesture, tossed it to Julius, who set it on his head.

The crowd gradually became quiet to hear the Emperor's citation.

"You have done well," he said, for all to hear.

There was a brief silence, and then the shouts broke out again.

"Free him! Free him! Free him!"

Caesar raised his arms. His face was now dark with frustration and rage. But he uttered the words and fifty thousand spectators heard them.

"You are a free man."

The crowd broke into renewed cheers, this time of approval for the Emperor's decision. And while they cheered, the Emperor summoned the gladiators.

Julius, in a haze of joy and relief, watched them entering the ring – six of them, massive, their brass armour and drawn swords harshly glittering in the sunlight, their face-concealing helmets giving them an inhuman look. Were they going to fight each other in three pairs? Why were they coming in now, before the tigers had gone back to their cages?

Suddenly Julius saw the Emperor point, first to one tiger, then to the other, and turn his thumb down. Three at a time, the armoured giants bore down on Boots and Brute.

"No! *NO!*"

Julius heard her voice, clear and shrill above the quietening crowd.

"Don't hurt them!" she cried, and now they all heard her. "Don't punish the tigers, the beautiful ones! Let them live!"

Caesar's thumb jabbed downward again. He was going to take his revenge on the beasts for his defeat and humiliation.

But the crowd would have none of it. The great

concourse of people had the power now and they sensed it. They would not permit the tigers to be put to death! Not after this! There was the thrill of bloodshed, but this – this unique performance – was a thrill of another kind. This was conquest by will and courage, and besides, the tigers must live to fight and give them pleasure another day.

A single male voice took up the princess's cry.

"Show mercy, Great Caesar! Spare the tigers!"

And again the roar of the crowd deafened Julius and defeated Caesar's intention. The gladiators, uncertain, stopped in their tracks and turned to the Royal Box, waiting for instructions. The Emperor's arm was still extended, but as the people's chanting roars battered him in waves, the sinews twisted, the fist slowly reversed itself. The thumb turned upwards.

Objects began to rain down on to the sand as the people threw flowers, laurels, coins, pieces of jewellery, articles of clothing. The crowd was hysterical in its delight, reinforced by a sense of its own power. There was not one person in the crowd who did not realise that they had overcome Caesar's strongest intentions, that their mass will had triumphed.

Something hard – a sandal – struck Brute on the flank.

He leapt up, and, alarmed by this sudden rain of missiles, fled toward Boots, leaving a trail of blood. They drew together. Julius watched them. Now they were pressed to each other, side to side. *Do they remember they are brothers?* Did it matter? They were the same species – it was tigers against men. Two against a vast mob that must seem to them like one great animal, menacing them from above and from all around.

This was the way of it, Julius realised. However strong, however fierce an animal, however bravely it fought, it was never enough in the arena. In the end, the forces of man could always win. Man, the absolute master of what the world produces. The heartless conqueror.

The injustice of it! The cruelty of it! And it was the same with Rome. None could stand against its power – the power of the Caesars.

Julius felt a great heat rising in him as he looked at the two tigers huddled together, cowering, gazing in fear at the gladiators standing ready to inflict death at the order of Caesar. Yet a moment ago, Caesar had suffered a defeat – had been turned from his purpose by his own people, any one of whom, individually, he could have had killed without thought or scruple.

He could still have Julius killed.

Julius, looking up at him in his own moment of victory – of freedom! He was no longer a slave! – with the people's plaudits ringing in his ears, knew that he might still be a dead man. That when the arena was cleared and the people had gone home, when the tigers were back in their cages, Caesar could send some agent to seek Julius out and murder him.

Yes. He would be capable of that. Of freeing Julius, and then wiping him out like a hated stain.

Julius gave one burning look at Aurelia. Their eyes met, and there it was – he saw it. He saw love for him shining from her eyes. Love that at last he could feel he had earned. And as if to prove it, she snatched the *palla* from her shoulders and, rolling it up to give it substance, she threw it down to him. He caught it on the point of his sword. Under the furious eyes of Caesar, he draped it around his neck and raised his arm to her. It was like a blown kiss, and Caesar went white to the lips.

The crowd, however, loved the gestures, and went completely mad.

And so, it seemed, did Julius.

The feel of the warm silk on the skin of his neck banished all traces of fear. He turned on his heel from the Royal Box, and strode towards the tigers, where they stood huddled together, frightened, cowed. He put his hands on their heads – yes, on Brute's too, and Brute submitted. Julius backed away, calling them, beckoning in the special way that Boots understood. Boots came, and his brother, not to be abandoned, followed.

The newly freed man took them out of the arena through the one opening that led, not down into the cellars, but out on to the streets of Rome.

No one stopped them. In that great arena, so wondrously constructed that it could be emptied of its many thousand spectators in a few minutes, doors were easily opened. The guards on the outer gate saw a man emerge, and moved to intercept him – and then came two tigers, walking side by side, unrestrained... The guards shrank instinctively, unable to hold their posts, and then as the beasts came nearer, dropped their spears and fled.

Julius stood, looking about him at the empty streets under the hot noonday sun. The tigers stood before him, as if waiting for his command. Behind them, over the top of the high, curved perimeter wall, the crowd could still be heard, baying its approval.

Julius knew he had only minutes before Caesar realised what had happened – that they had passed out of the Colosseum to freedom instead of into the cellars where they belonged. Pursuit would be swift and deadly. They must escape – all of them! But Julius dared not run ahead of the tigers – Brute would remember himself and give chase. The tigers must go first.

"Go, my beauties! Go!" he cried.

For a moment the two animals stood, uncertain, afraid. Then Boots took the lead. He had been free before. He knew these streets, he knew the route to freedom. He turned his head to his brother. Julius saw and understood the communication that passed between them. *Follow. We go together.*

Then he bounded away.

Brute sprang after him. His wound hampered him – he stumbled – but recovered. In a double swirl of black and gold, they rounded a corner and were lost to sight.

And now Julius, too, ran. He threw the heavy sword away. He must get to his mother, bid her goodbye. He would leave his laurels with her. Then he must do as the tigers would do – run to the edge of the city and away to the unpeopled wild country to the south.

Alone, friendless, pursued, his love left behind him for ever. But free.

EPILOGUE

Aurelia never saw Julius again.

Her father did not punish her any more. His defeat at the hands of the crowd weighed more strongly on him; he couldn't blame her for that. And besides, with barbarians threatening the Empire, he had many affairs of state to deal with that quite turned his mind from the events in the Colosseum that day. Father and daughter were never again close. But the Emperor had no further cause to complain of Aurelia's disobedience.

Two years later, she consented to marry her cousin Marcus. The marriage being an arranged match, romantic love was not part of it. Nevertheless, it was not unhappy. The two understood each other at a deep level, and remained good companions. In later life, a mixture of blessings and misfortunes drew them ever closer together.

They had four children. Two of them, who showed signs of defects, quietly died in infancy, whether in the course of nature or with some assistance is not certain. The other two, a boy and a girl, were exceptionally beautiful and brilliant, seeming to have inherited the finest qualities, in looks and character, of their parents. And the two sister-grandmothers, who had engineered the match between their closely related children and had then suffered agonies of doubt and guilt, drew breath again.

Both Aurelia's older brothers died before their father, one in battle, and one in mysterious circumstances, a fate that befell a number of heirs to the Caesars down the centuries. So the next emperor was Aurelia's and Marcus's second son. His name was Secundus Darius, but when he assumed the mantle of Caesar after the death of his grandfather, he fulfilled his mother's wish and changed his name to Julius Secundus.

Julius Secundus ruled well, and it was in his time that the circus began to play a less prominent part in the life of Rome. It still took place, but this Caesar's thumb was more often turned up than down, and the number of animals imported to service the arena was far lower. This was partly because Rome's power and reach were on the wane. The incursions of barbarian tribes from the north and east became more frequent, and the cost of defending the far-flung borders of the Empire became ever more impossible to maintain. Those borders began to shrink, and thus the power of Rome to crumble.

Christianity was taking hold stealthily but steadily. Though it would be years yet before the Emperor Constantine yielded to his mother's wishes and declared Christianity the official religion of Rome, Aurelia was able to cleave to her new beliefs – although in secret – and teach them to her children, though they could not practise openly.

She never persuaded her nurse, however, who clung to the old gods till her death. Even as she lay dying, though much tempted, she never told Aurelia how she had paid Caius to have a sword put into Julius's hand, or how she felt when Caius had not lived long enough to spend her bribe... She took to her grave the secret of the vital part she had played on the day Julius had triumphed, been freed, and disappeared for ever.

And what became of the two tigers?

Who can say for certain? They were never caught. Large tracts of southern Italy at that time were unpopulated, full of game and places of concealment.

It's entirely possible that they lived out their lives in that wild country, rediscovering their true nature after their years of captivity. It's pleasant to imagine the brothers becoming reacquainted, hunting, sleeping and playing together as they roamed free across those stony, broken hills and warm, sheltered valleys. One may imagine a combination of talents – Brute's for the chase, Boots's for concealment. One might fear for Rufus, the thieving, simple shepherd, if his path crossed theirs!

But surely Boots could never have become a man-eater.

And Julius?

Loneliness is not a problem for two brother tigers together. But what of a young man who has left behind all that he knows and loves, never to be recovered?

It's good to think he may have made his way south down the long leg of Italy and found human companionship in a village or small hill town, safely remote from the capital. He could have pretended to be a wandering storyteller. And what a story of romance and daring he could have told, without straying from the truth! The slowly fading silk scarf he always wore about his neck would give rise to many questions.

But if he was wise, as surely he grew to be, he would not tell his true story, but others that would need some wit to invent, and thus earn his bread and keep his true past a secret, as he kept his first love, deep in his heart.

Author's Note

There were many Roman emperors, but the one in this story is invented, as are the other characters, and all the events told here are fictitious.

However, as nearly as possible, the facts about ancient Rome – the way people lived, the Colosseum, the role of animals and fighters in the circus, the often despotic rule of the Caesars after the original democratic ideas of early Rome had been abandoned, and the slow, secret growth of Christianity – these are all as true as I can make them.

I have purposely not given any exact date, but if you think of the late third century A.D. – about two hundred years of slow decline before the Roman Empire fell and was replaced by the Greek, or Byzantine – that would be about right.

Stealing Stacey

All my helpless, angry thoughts
suddenly came together to form one word.
One answer.
Australia.
On the other side of the world.
An escape from everything…

Stacey's life in London really sucks.
Then, out of the blue, a glamorous gran she's never
met comes to visit – all the way from Australia.
When Stacey gets the worst news yet, Grandma
Glendine offers her the perfect solution.

0-00-715922-6

HarperCollins *Children's Books*

www.harpercollinschildrensbooks.co.uk

THE
INDIAN
IN THE
CUPBOARD

Lynne Reid Banks

Neither Omri nor the Indian moved for perhaps a minute and a half. They hardly breathed either. They just stared at each other.

At first, Omri is unimpressed with the plastic Indian toy he is given for his birthday. But when he puts it in his old cupboard and turns the key, something extraordinary happens that will change Omri's life for ever. For Little Bull, the Iroquois Indian brave, comes to life…

The first book in the magical series about
Omri and Little Bull

0-00-714898-4

HarperCollins *Children's Books*

www.harpercollinschildrensbooks.co.uk

RETURN
OF THE
INDIAN

Lynne Reid Banks

...Lying face-down across the pony's back was a limp, motionless form. It was Little Bull.

Omri can't resist bringing the small people back to life again. But when the cupboard door opens, Omri finds Little Bull unconscious with two bullet wounds in his back. As Omri tries to help him, he faces the terrifying responsibility of power – the power of life and death...

The second book in the magical series about
Omri and Little Bull

0-00-714899-2

HarperCollins *Children's Books*

www.harpercollinschildrensbooks.co.uk